DANCE
OF
LIFE

DANCE
OF
LIFE

•

Ilsa Mayr

AVALON BOOKS
NEW YORK

© Copyright 2003 by Ilse Dallmayr
Library of Congress Catalog Card Number: 2003090549
ISBN 0-8034-9602-8

Published by Thomas Bouregy & Co., Inc.
160 Madison Avenue, New York, NY 10016

PRINTED IN THE UNITED STATES OF AMERICA
ON ACID-FREE PAPER
BY HADDON CRAFTSMEN, BLOOMSBURG, PENNSYLVANIA

With many thanks to my faithful, supportive, perceptive
critique group members
(in alphabetical order):
Amy, Cheryl, Joanna, Laura, Mellanie, Phyllis.

Chapter One

"One more outburst from you, Samantha Josephine Crawford, and you'll spend the weekend in county jail."

"But—"

"Not another word."

Seeing the judge's expression, Sammi Jo snapped her mouth shut, sat down, and fumed. She clenched her hands so that her fingernails dug into her palms. The pain kept her from telling Andy Rafe just what she thought of him. Who did he think he was, telling her to be quiet! Sammi Jo took two deep breaths. Losing her temper wouldn't help.

Who'd have thought that Andy Rafe, prince of the nerds at Robert E. Lee High School, would end up being His Honor, Judge Andrew Raiford Garroway? And that he would be in a position to tell her what to do? Worse, that he would have power over her, and worse yet, enjoy having power over her? Life was full of unpleasant surprises.

"I'm ordering you to perform two hundred hours of

1

community service," the judge said and rapped his gavel.

Sammi Jo opened her mouth to protest, but when her attorney kicked her under the table, she swallowed her angry words.

"The alternative is thirty days in county jail."

Jail? Sammi Jo felt faint. At the same time, blood roared in her ears, drowning out her attorney's response. After a few minutes, Dinah Farnsworth grabbed Sammi Jo's arm and hustled her out of the courtroom and into the nearest ladies' room.

"He can't do this to me! At first he said one hundred hours and now it's two hundred? Tell me he can't do this?" Sammi Jo pleaded with her attorney.

"I'm afraid he can, and he has. You can't talk back to a judge. You're lucky he didn't hold you in contempt."

Sammi Jo bristled. "He is not so lucky. I hold him in contempt. He acts like somebody appointed him lord of the universe. Maybe he's fooled everyone else into thinking he's different, but he hasn't fooled me. Deep down he's still the nerd he always was."

"That's a little harsh, isn't it?" Dinah asked.

"Making me do two hundred hours for taking part in that protest march is more than a little harsh."

"A protest march that got out of hand," the attorney added meaningfully. "And you fought and kicked that police officer."

"He grabbed me! In a way I'm sure the police academy didn't teach him to grab a woman. I'd have kicked any man who touched me like that uninvited."

Sammi Jo splashed cold water on her face. After she dabbed it dry with a paper towel, she felt more calm. She took a deep breath and addressed her attorney. "Where am I going to find the time to do that much community service? I'm trying to get my dance studio going, and I'm taking care of my grandfather. There aren't enough hours now to get everything done that I have to do. How can I add all that community service on top of everything else?"

Dinah laid a hand on Sammi Jo's arm. "Judge Garroway hasn't said yet how quickly you have to perform this service. Let me see what I can work out. It wouldn't hurt to write a note of apology."

Sammi Jo groaned.

"If we can get the two hundred hours spread out over a year or more, wouldn't that help?"

Reluctantly and still a little resentfully, Sammi Jo muttered, "Okay, I'll write the note."

The attorney studied her client. "I've been in Judge Garroway's court many times, and I've never seen anyone ruffle his feathers. What's between you two? How well and how long have you known him?"

"Since middle school. I was in seventh grade, and he was in eighth, but we were in the same Spanish class."

"And?"

Sammi Jo shrugged but remained silent.

"You got under his skin. There's got to be more in your shared past than being in the same class."

"When I was a junior and he a senior, he helped me with algebra-trig. Andy Rafe wouldn't accept money for the tutoring. Instead, he wanted me to go to the prom with him. Since he kept me from flunking that math class, I said I'd go."

"And?"

"And I stood him up."

In the silence that followed her statement, Sammi

Jo felt her face grow hot. Feeling guilty and defensive, even after all these years, she said, "I'm not proud of standing him up, of having given in to my parents' pressure, but for heaven's sake, that was twelve years ago! Who cares anymore what happened in high school. It was all ridiculous kids' stuff."

"I agree that the cliques were ridiculous, but those of us who weren't the cheerleaders or the jocks or the preps, we still remember, and deep down a lot of us still mind having been excluded."

Sammi Jo stared at her attorney, truly astonished. Here was a successful, well-off, professional woman who still seemed to mind not having belonged to a popular clique. As if belonging to the so-called "in" groups had been all fun and games.

"I know this is dumb, but part of me still minds not being considered good enough to belong to the in group." Dinah shrugged. "We're all products of our past. None of us can escape that."

"I've never thought about what it must have been like to be excluded. I'm sorry," Sammi Jo said. Had she been so self-absorbed that she never wondered about those who had been excluded?

Thinking back, Sammi Jo remembered worrying about getting decent grades, making the cheerleading squad, taking piano lessons, being thin and pretty enough to please her ex–beauty queen mother and ever critical father, and never having enough time to pursue her one true love—dancing. Whatever she had been, it hadn't been self-absorbed. She had been too busy trying to live up to everyone else's expectations.

"Did you go to the prom with someone else?" Dinah asked, interrupting Sammi Jo's long silence.

"No. I wasn't that insensitive. I stayed home and

pretended to be sick. Actually, I didn't have to pretend to be sick, not after the fight I had with my dad."

"Let me guess. You were popular. A member of the in crowd, and Andrew Garroway wasn't. Right?"

"Right." Sammi Jo closed her eyes and rubbed her left temple wearily where a her head was beginning to throb. "That's all so long ago, and so much has happened since then. I can hardly remember the girl I was. Andy Rafe's a judge now. Surely he's not letting something like a missed prom influence his decision."

Her attorney was silent for a moment. Then she said, "I don't think so. He's one of the most impartial judges I know. But write that note anyway."

Sammi Jo promised she would.

At ten-thirty that night Sammi Jo unlocked the front door of her grandfather's house. Light spilled from the open door of his bedroom. Sammi Jo hurried toward it.

"Granddad, are you all right?"

"I'm fine. I wasn't sleepy, so I thought I'd read for a while."

Sammi Jo looked at the tall figure in the wheelchair. As always, his silver-white hair was neatly brushed, his mustache trimmed, his robe carefully tied. Though pale, her grandfather didn't seem to be in pain. She dropped her gym bag and collapsed into the chair next to his bed.

"You look all done in, Sugar. Busy day?"

Before she could answer, her stomach growled loudly.

"You didn't eat dinner again," Nate said with a fierce frown.

"Today I really didn't have time. Going to court this morning made me run late all day."

"Are you still as upset as you were when you phoned me?"

"No. There's no point in staying upset. What's done is done." She shrugged, exhausted. "Anyway, I'm going to the kitchen to see if I can find something to eat. Keep me company?"

"There are some of the chili beans left I fixed."

Sammi Jo shook her head. "No, thanks. I always expect flames to shoot out of my mouth when I eat your chili beans."

Her grandfather chuckled as he followed her into the kitchen. "If you don't break out in a sweat, the chili's not worth eating."

"I've sweated plenty today, thank you, leading four aerobics classes on top of my regular schedule. I want something cool and soothing."

"Sounds like a tall, cold one to me," Nate said wistfully.

Sammi Jo started to remind her grandfather what the doctor had said about drinking beer, then changed her mind. He had already given up steaks, cigars, and bourbon. An occasional beer wouldn't kill him. She had come to the conclusion that the quality of life was as important as the quantity. Maybe even more important. Sammi Jo took a lager from the fridge, opened it, and handed it to him. When she noted his surprised expression, she winked at him and said, "Enjoy."

"Thanks, Sugar. Join me?"

"Some other time. Right now I need something with vitamins in it." She poured herself a tall glass of vegetable juice, spread peanut butter onto one long celery stalk and hummus onto another, stirred wheat germ, ground flax seeds, and chopped walnuts into a carton of yogurt, took a package of whole wheat crackers from the cupboard, and brought everything to the kitchen table.

Nate rolled his wheelchair to the table and watched her, his expression affectionately tolerant.

"What?" Sammi Jo asked between crunchy bites of celery.

"The things you eat. Whatever happened to a plate-ful of meat and potatoes? I can't eat like that anymore because of my heart, but you're young and healthy and must burn thousands of calories in your work. You're not trying to get skinnier, are you?" he asked, his voice disapproving.

"No. Though if my ex-husband saw me now, he would undoubtedly tell me with great glee that I was getting fat. He was always reminding me how many calories there were in everything I ate."

"I don't understand. Why would he think you're getting fat?"

"Because I'm a dress size larger and lots more mus-cular since I've divorced him. Must be the weight training I've added to my routine. I feel strong and healthy."

"Your ex-husband always was a great, big, dumb jerk."

"I wish someone had told me that before I married him. Would have saved me a lot of trouble and dis-appointment."

"Would you have listened if I'd said he was a jerk?"

Sammi Jo thought about it for a moment. "Probably not. Getting married at the time seemed the right thing to do." She stirred the yogurt, her thoughts on past choices, past opportunities. "If I had to do it over, knowing what I know now, I'd never get married."

"Just because you had one bad experience with matrimony doesn't mean a second marriage would be bad too. Your grandmother, rest her soul, and I were happily married for fifty-two years."

"With my luck, I'd marry another great, big, dumb jerk. No, I'm better off by myself. As soon as my dance studio is making a profit, I won't have to teach so many aerobics classes and life will be easier. Even more important, I'll have more time to train for dance competitions and life will be more fun." Sammi Jo stopped, then, remembering her court appearance, her mood plummeted.

"Why the dark expression?" Nate asked.

"I just remembered the two hundred hours of community service that nerd assigned to me. I still can't believe he did that."

"Are you talking about Judge Garroway?"

Surprise caused Sammi Jo to lower her spoon. "Do you know him?"

"Sure. We play chess once a week. He's a good player. A worthy opponent. Why do you call him a nerd? Because he wasn't part of your crowd in high school?"

Sammi Jo shrugged.

"Well, he certainly is part of this town's movers and shakers now." When his granddaughter looked stunned, Nate added, "A person can change a lot in twelve years. You have. Don't you think Andrew can?"

"I suppose so," Sammi Jo admitted. It would take a drastic change in her thinking to see Andy Rafe in a new way. Perhaps she could start by referring to him as Andrew.

"So tell me about Andrew Garroway, the mover and shaker. Isn't he a little young to be a judge?" she asked.

"He's well qualified, despite his age. It wouldn't surprise me one bit if one of these days he sitting on the bench of the North Carolina Supreme Court. Maybe even of the U.S. Supreme Court."

"Is he ambitious?"

"I think so, but not in a ruthless way. You have goals and ambitions, and so does he."

"I wasn't faulting him for being ambitious." There was a difference between wanting to get ahead, to achieve something, and the kind of blind, ruthless ambition that sacrificed personal relationships. Hadn't she paid the price for her ex-husband's ravenous appetites and ambitions? Sammi Jo dismissed the dark, bitter feeling that still filled her when she thought of the empty, wasted years of her marriage.

"Does the judge have a family?" she asked.

"He's not married, if that's what you're wondering about."

"I wasn't." Sammi Jo avoided meeting her grandfather's gaze, since that was exactly what she'd been curious about.

"Not that he couldn't have his pick of women, according to Mrs. Pruitt."

"Mrs. Pruitt? How does your cleaning lady know that?" Sammi Jo asked.

"She cleans for Andrew as well. Besides, have you forgotten that everyone in Pine Springs knows everything about everyone else? According to Mrs. Pruitt, Andrew is considered quite the catch of the county.

Women are always phoning him and leaving messages and invitations. She, of course, disapproves of such forward behavior."

Trying to visualize Andy Rafe as a good catch entailed a giant leap in her imagination. When she had known him, he wasn't even considered a desirable date. At least not by her friends and her parents. If she ever came face to face with him again, she would have to take a second look.

Nate downed the last of his beer. "That hit the spot. I think I'll finish reading my chapter and then go to bed."

Sammi Jo glanced at the thick book resting in her grandfather's lap. "*Lee and Grant*. Are you restaging the recent unpleasantness between the states?" she asked teasingly.

"Don't be fresh, Missy. I've never referred to the Civil War that way. My daddy did, though," Nate admitted with a grin. "Are you staying up?"

"Only long enough to write a note."

Sammi Jo had a sinking feeling that the note to Andy Rafe wouldn't be easy to write.

Four days later Sammi Jo's attorney phoned to tell her that Judge Garroway had given her twenty months in which to complete the community service.

"Works out to about two-and-a-half hours per week. That's a very generous time line, don't you agree?" Dinah asked.

"I suppose so."

"Why the reluctance to admit that Judge Garroway was generous?"

"I'm remembering how generous he was when he ordered me to serve two hundred hours," Sammi Jo said, her voice tinged with resentment. Then, resolutely suppressing her lingering bad feelings, she said, "But there's no point in complaining. Where am I to serve my time, and what am I going to be doing?"

"Teaching ballroom dancing at the community center."

Sammi Jo was speechless for a moment. "Pine Springs, North Carolina, has a community center?"

"Yes. I guess you haven't been back here often enough to know that."

"After my parents moved to Raleigh and my grandfather only spent his summers here, I didn't have any reason to return."

"The center is a nice place for teenagers."

"Teenagers? Andrew Garroway wants me to teach ballroom dancing to a bunch of teens? Are you sure he said *ballroom* dancing?"

"I'm sure."

"Holy hula! Hasn't he been around kids enough to know that learning to waltz isn't going to thrill them? He can't be that out of touch." She paused for a moment. "On the other hand, remembering how he always lived in a world of his own, he could be," Sammi Jo muttered.

"He said ballroom dancing would be good for them. A gentle, civilizing influence."

Sammi Jo rolled her eyes. Did Andy Rafe visualize her teaching them the Viennese waltz and the cotillion?

"Are you still there?" Dinah asked.

"Yes, I'm still here." Sammi Jo's mind raced. Ballroom dancing wasn't just classic waltzes and sedate fox-trots. Did His Honor realize that swing, the rumba, the cha-cha, the tango and the paso dobles, all dances with some fun and very, very sexy moves, were considered ballroom dancing too?

"Can you do it?" Dinah asked.

"Of course I can do it. I was trying to imagine the logistics."

"You're to call the director and he'll help you set it up. You know, put flyers out, sign the kids up, pick a time."

"How soon do I have to start?"

"Next week."

Sammi Jo gulped. "What's his hurry? Doesn't he realize how much planning this will involve? That I'll have to reschedule some private lessons?"

"I know this will cause you some inconveniences, but after the judge gave us twenty months, I didn't feel I could push for a delay. Can't you have an organizational meeting first? I'm sure that would count toward the two hundred hours and would meet the requirement of starting next week."

"I like the way you lawyers think."

Dinah chuckled. "One more thing. Twice a month you have to report your progress and the number of hours of community work completed."

"All right. To whom do I report my progress?"

"To the judge."

"To him personally?"

"Yes. Judge Garroway takes his duties seriously."

It was on the tip of Sammi Jo's tongue to suggest that the judge should get a life, but she restrained herself. Before she could say anything, Dinah spoke again.

"Call his secretary and make an appointment."

"That man sure is cutting into my time," Sammi Jo grumbled.

* * *

When the doorbell rang on Monday evening, Sammi Jo looked at the clock with a frown. She wasn't expecting anyone. It couldn't be her grandfather returning from his physical therapy. He always had the van drop him off at the back door, which was the only one equipped with a ramp for his wheelchair. Maybe it was Lavinia, their next-door neighbor, stopping in for a chat.

Sammi Jo dried her hands on a kitchen towel and dashed to the front door. When she opened it, the polite words of greeting died on her lips. She stared at the man facing her for several beats before she could speak.

"You! What are you doing here?"

Andrew raised an eyebrow. "Is that a way to greet a visitor? You sound downright surly. Your mother would be appalled by your lack of graciousness."

She crossed her arms over her chest. "My mother isn't here, and I don't feel gracious toward you. What are you going to do? Hold me in contempt and add another hundred hours of community service to my sentence?"

Sammi Jo almost gasped when she saw his reaction. The irritating man had the audacity to grin at her. And an appealing grin it was at that. She didn't remember Andy Rafe having that kind of a smile.

"Are you going to ask me in?" he inquired, his tone mild.

"Why? So you can tell me I have to illustrate that written report your secretary said I had to submit? Diagram the dance steps I'll be teaching?"

"Now there's a thought."

"Don't you even—"

"Relax, Sammi Jo. I was only kidding."

Odd. She didn't remember Andy Rafe having a sense of humor. She looked at him suspiciously. Maybe her grandfather was right. Maybe the man had changed drastically.

"I'm here to see your grandfather. It's our chess night. We play every Monday evening," Andrew explained.

"Oh. He didn't tell me. And he's not back yet from his physical therapy."

"I'm a few minutes early. May I come in now?"

Sammi Jo hesitated for a moment before a lifetime of good manners took over. "I'm sorry. Of course." She stepped aside to let him enter. As he passed by, she caught the scent he wore—something subtle and expensive and most pleasant. Possibly the scent her ex-husband had asked her to buy him for his birthday, only the marriage had fallen apart before that day arrived.

"Something smells good," Andrew said.

"Pardon?" she asked, appalled. How could Andy Rafe know she'd been thinking about how great he smelled?

"Are you cooking something?"

"Yes. Oh, good grief!" Sammi Jo ran to the kitchen where she snatched a pan off the burner. "Just in time." She turned the flame down.

Andrew glanced at his watch. "Are you just now fixing dinner? Maybe Nate forgot about our game."

"We've eaten. This is part of tomorrow's dinner. Now that I've been charged with civilizing Pine Springs' teenagers through ballroom dancing, I have to budget my time carefully." Sammi Jo shot him one of her severe looks which left him totally unfazed. "Will you answer a question?"

"Depends, but ask it anyway," he replied.

"I've checked around. You didn't give any of the other protesters two hundred hours of community service. Why me?"

"None of them sassed the judge."

"Don't you mean that none of them stood up the judge twelve years ago?" she snapped.

"You think this is about revenge?"

"Isn't it?"

"No, it isn't! It's about the dignity of the court, of the law, of justice. What do you think would happen if I allowed every crook who faces the bench to be disrespectful and flaunt the rules? Anarchy and disaster, that's what. The court calendar is way too crowded as it is without wasting time on reprimands."

Judging by his impassioned tone, she seemed to have struck a nerve. "Didn't you overreact just a little bit?"

"No, I didn't."

"I think you did. You could have made your point without doubling my hours of community service. You didn't have to come down on me like the proverbial ton of bricks!"

"What did you think I'd do? Let you slide the way everyone always has because you're beautiful and charming and come from one of the town's leading families? Because you were the golden girl of Robert E. Lee High School and everybody adored you?"

"What?" Sammi Jo heard her voice squeak. When she tried to speak again, her throat felt so tight she had to swallow twice and take a couple of breaths.

"Let me slide? Is that what you think happened?

That I've never had to work at anything? That I've coasted along on family connections and a particular combination of genes, skin, and bones?" Sammi Jo paused for a breath again. She had to. Her lungs couldn't seem to function normally. She thought she'd hyperventilate. Anger always did that to her. Or made her cry, which was even worse. She'd rather die than let Andy Rafe see her cry.

"Sammi Jo, wait—"

"You wait." She grabbed the edge of the table to keep from hurling herself at him and inflicting serious physical damage on his judicial body. "How dare you think that everything's been handed to me?" she asked, her voice vibrating with fury.

"How dare you think I'm after revenge?"

They glowered at each other, separated by the kitchen table, until the ringing of the phone split the charged, heated silence. Sammi Jo let it ring and ring, not trusting herself to speak.

"Aren't you going to answer that?" Andy Rafe finally asked.

Sammi Jo flicked him one last slit-eyed look before she snatched up the receiver and barked a hello. "Oh sorry, Granddad. Where are you?" She listen to her grandfather's voice, all the while conscious of Andy Rafe's hot hazel eyes watching her like a falcon. "He's already here. Want to speak to him?" She glowered at the judge. "Okay, I'll tell him." She replaced the receiver.

"My grandfather's physical therapy ran late, but he should be home in about fifteen minutes. He'd appreciate it if you waited. In the meantime I'm supposed to . . ." Sammi Jo's voice trailed off.

"In the meantime you're supposed to do what?" Andrew prompted.

Sammi Jo couldn't get the words out. Blast and triple blast her grandfather's sense of hospitality. She watched Andy Rafe lean against the kitchen counter and cross his arms over his chest. And a nice, wide chest it was above a trim waist. She didn't remember him looking as if he worked out.

"What is it Nate wants you to do?" he asked with a hint of amusement in his voice.

He appeared perfectly at ease. Almost as if he were enjoying himself. She'd rather teach the conga to a cobra than entertain Andy Rafe. But she had no choice. For one thing, she was brought up to be polite to a visitor, and for another, she hated to disappoint her grandfather. He was the one person who had always loved her unconditionally.

Sammi Jo unclenched her teeth just enough to speak. "Fix you a cup of coffee and keep you company until he comes home."

Chapter Two

Twelve years ago Sammi Jo had been able to tie his insides into bloody knots with a mere glance from those stunning blue eyes. Now *he* could rattle *her*.

The sweet, heady feeling of satisfaction lasted for only a second before Andrew reminded himself how childish his reaction was. Hadn't he just claimed that he wasn't after revenge? And he wasn't. But he was human enough to feel just a twinge of gratification, and once in a while, even a judge was allowed to be human.

"Would you like a cup of coffee?" Sammi Jo asked.

Andrew noticed how hard she was trying to make her voice and expression gracious even though she would probably prefer to tell him to go jump into the lake behind her grandfather's house.

"I'd love a *good* cup of coffee."

Sammi Jo raised a delicately arched eyebrow. "Are you doubting I can make decent coffee?" she demanded.

Andrew shrugged. "No offense, but judging by the

18

lousy coffee that's usually served in Pine Springs, I'd have to say that chances of getting a decent cup are remote."

"Brace yourself then. You're in for a treat."

He watched her take a bag from the refrigerator, grind the beans and place them and filtered water into a fancy-looking coffeemaker. She was serious about her coffee.

Sammi Jo moved her dancer's body with grace, control, and ease, but then, she always had. As a teenager she had been slender, so slender that she had appeared almost breakable. Her fragility had intensified the aura of unapproachability she radiated and had caused him to feel even more clumsy and awkward than nature had made him. Now, though still slender, she looked strong and athletic. A man wouldn't have to be afraid of holding her.

Whoa. Why was he thinking of holding her? Hadn't he wasted his teenage years dreaming of doing just that? He was now a mature man and way beyond obsessing about holding an unattainable woman in his arms—even if the woman were Sammi Jo Crawford.

While the coffee dripped through the filter, Sammi Jo chopped tomatoes, which she added to the onions and garlic in the pot she'd rescued earlier from the heat. Though he had made himself a tuna sandwich at six o'clock, the tantalizing smell filling the kitchen made him hungry again.

"The way you chop those vegetables reminds me of that chef on television. Where did you learn to do that?"

"At a cooking institute."

"You studied cooking?"

"Why not? I had to do something. I can't stand to

play golf or bridge more than once a week. And I enjoy cooking. If my dancing school doesn't succeed, I can always get a job as a chef."

"You've been divorced for what? Two years?"

"Yes."

"You taught dancing in Atlanta after your divorce?"

"Yes."

"Nate never mentioned having great-grandchildren," Andrew said casually.

"That's because he doesn't have any."

The way she answered him and the way she halved that zucchini with one chop of the cleaver told him to drop the other questions he was dying to ask about her marriage and her ex-husband. The wedding photo in the newspaper had made them look like the perfect couple everyone had said they were. What had happened? Andrew thought it prudent to bide his time. Once they knew each other better, she might feel freer to talk about her past.

"I think it's a nice thing you're doing for your grandfather." When she looked at him questioningly, he added, "I mean, giving up your job in Atlanta and coming to Pine Springs to take care of him."

"I was ready for a change, and I've always felt closest to my grandfather. Coming back was no sacrifice. Of course, I didn't know I'd run afoul of the law almost immediately when I got back. Or that I'd get the strictest judge in the state to preside over my case."

Sammi Jo didn't sound angry anymore. For an instant he thought he detected a teasing light in the look she leveled at him. When she glanced at him again, her eyes were serious. He must have imagined that teasing light. Still, her lack of anger was progress.

When she diced a cube of some white substance, he asked, "What's that?"

"Tofu."

He leaned forward for a better look. "So that's what the stuff looks like."

"You've never had tofu?"

"No. What's it taste like?"

"Like nothing. It takes on the flavors of the food around it." She crossed to the bay window and snipped several leaves off an herb plant. "Basil," she explained and lifted the leaves for him to sniff.

"Nice," Andrew murmured, meaning the herb as well as the fragrance of Sammi Jo's hair. He hadn't been this close to her in twelve years, and glory be, she was still utterly beautiful. Breathtakingly beautiful with skin as flawless and fine-grained as heirloom porcelain, hair that shimmered like pure gold, and features that were as perfect as those of a classical sculpture. No wonder men grew slack-jawed and weak-kneed in her presence.

"By the time I'm through adding spices, the tofu will taste as Italian as mozzarella."

"Your grandfather told me you put him on this special diet. No more fried catfish, barbecued ribs, or steak."

"Doctor's orders. He's recovering well. We don't want to risk a second stroke. I'm not claiming that he likes the new way he has to eat, but he's beginning to accept it without muttering unkind words after each bite."

Andrew chuckled. "I can see him doing it. Muttering just loud enough to let you know he's doing it, but too low to understand what he's saying. He does that sometimes when we play chess."

"You don't get him too excited, do you?" Sammi Jo asked with a worried frown.

"No. Ours are nice, relaxing games."

"Good. He has to watch his blood pressure." Sammi Jo looked at the coffee. "Ready to risk drinking a cup?"

"I am if you are."

"How do you take yours?"

"Black."

She nodded in approval. "The only time I add sugar or milk is when the coffee is too awful to drink straight." Sammi Jo ignored the serviceable mugs sitting on the counter, took two delicate china cups from the glass-fronted cabinet, and filled them with coffee. "Do you mind drinking it in here? I really need to get this pasta sauce ready."

"Not at all. I like this kitchen," he said, looking around. And what was there not to like? A beautiful woman moved gracefully over the brick floor, white appliances gleamed next to warm maple cabinets, the air was filled with the aroma of good food cooking, of coffee brewing, of fragrant herbs in the window, of some delicate-smelling blue flowers in a white vase on the table. Andrew felt almost light-headed as his senses absorbed the various sensations. Only now did he realize how austere his life was, how starved his senses were for stimulation.

"At least sit down," Sammi Jo said, handing him a cup.

"I'd rather stand and watch you cook."

"Suit yourself."

Sammi Jo lifted the cup and inhaled the scent of the coffee before she took a sip. Then she watched him and waited for his verdict.

Andrew sniffed, took a sip, and closed his eyes. "I think I've died and gone to coffee heaven," he murmured.

"So you like it?"

"I like it a lot. Great aroma, good dark color, rich smooth taste. If I'd known that you could make such good coffee, I'd have rethought your community service assignment. Might have assigned you to brewing the courthouse coffee each morning. We'd all be in a better mood if we had decent coffee."

"Who's we?"

"My staff, and everyone from the security guard at the entrance to the clerks and the district attorney and his people. About twenty-five or so coffee drinkers."

"It's not hard to make great coffee. All you need is a good coffeemaker and some quality beans. Why don't you make it? Or is it beneath the dignity of a judge to make the morning coffee?"

Andrew shrugged, his expression a little sheepish. "I never thought about making it. Seems that from the time I get to my chambers till I leave at night, there isn't a quiet moment."

"And here I thought judges spent hours in Solomon-like solitude, pondering their decisions."

"I wish."

"This county never seemed to me to be a mecca of crime. Why are you so busy?"

"We may not have drive-by shootings or more than one or two murders a year, but we get our share of traffic violations, domestic disputes, Saturday night fights, petty theft, and the occasional trafficking in moonshine. Not to mention hotheaded environmental demonstrators."

Sammi Jo looked at him over the rim of her cup.

"If I were you, I'd watch out for those hotheaded demonstrators. They could be dangerous."

Wasn't that the truth. Especially when the demonstrator was a lissome, golden-haired dancer with long, sexy legs. Sammi Jo wore a green tank top and white shorts and though Andrew was a disciplined man who told himself not to stare at her legs like some desperate adolescent, his eyes kept disobeying his brain. To counteract his traitorous senses his mind reminded him that Sammi Jo had been a cruel, thoughtless girl, and that he had no evidence to think she had reformed.

According to Nate, it was Sammi Jo who had initiated the divorce proceedings. Andrew acknowledged that it was rarely only one partner's fault when a marriage broke up. Still, to have a woman like her walk out on a man had to be devastating. Part of him felt compassion for her husband, and part of him was glad that Sammi Jo was single and back in Pine Springs. When the contradiction of this thought hit him, he called himself a fool. He was a man of the law, used to reason and logic. To indulge in spurious, contradictory thinking was out of character. He frowned.

"What's the matter? I mentioned demonstrators and you look like a thundercloud dropped down on you. We weren't that bad, were we?"

That's how much she knew! Seeing her in his court had unnerved him, and he wasn't easily spooked. But a man didn't come face to face with his teenage fantasy girl every day. And that's all his current agitation was about—a reaction to an unexpected meeting. From now on every time he saw Sammi Jo he would undoubtedly be more and more his usual calm and collected self. By the time she finished her community service, he would hardly give her a second thought or look. That idea was enormously reassuring.

"Andy Rafe? Are you all right?"

"I'm fine. Why do you ask?"

"You've been quiet so long I thought you'd forgotten I was here."

Not yet, he hadn't.

"But then you often were off in a world of your own," she added.

"The computer nerd. Isn't that what your crowd called me?" He watched a pink blush color her fair skin.

"I always called you Andy Rafe. And you *were* a computer wizard. In your junior year, didn't you sell a game you designed for a lot of money? I'm surprised you didn't stick with computers."

"Designing programs was a good way to pay for college and law school, but I couldn't see myself spending my whole life doing that. It may be hard for you to believe, but I prefer people to machines."

Sammi Jo looked at him, puzzled. "Why would that be hard for me to believe?"

Andrew shrugged. "Remember, I was a bit of a loner. My social skills left a lot to be desired."

Sammi Jo quickly sifted through her high school memories, but she couldn't remember much about Andy Rafe. For one thing, he had been a year ahead of her, and for another, they hadn't run with the same crowd. Tactfully, she said, "I remember you as being brainy but a little shy."

"Is that your diplomatic way of saying I was a misfit?"

"Is that how you felt?"

"Objection. Now you're using a trial lawyer's tricks: answering a question with a question."

"Is that what they do? I'll have to ask Dinah about her other tricks of the trade. Anyway, we only spent time together during the second semester of my junior year when you kept me from flunking that math class. I really didn't know you well."

That hurt. Amazing how a few casual words could take such a lethal swipe at a man's ego. But Sammi Jo was right. Just because he had spent countless hours thinking and fantasizing about her didn't mean she had been more than barely aware that he existed.

"So, what do you do for entertainment in Pine Springs?" she asked.

Andrew risked a quick glance toward her. Luckily she hadn't noticed his disappointed reaction. Like a good hostess, she was making polite conversation. "Probably still the same things we did when you lived here."

Sammi Jo groaned. "I'm not sure I can take that much excitement. Back then this was the deadest town. Now at least there's a mall and a community center at which I'll be teaching ballroom dancing, thanks to you."

Andrew ignored her ironic thanks. "And we have Star Lake Resort."

"At which I'll also be teaching ballroom dancing."

"You will?"

"The social director needed some activity for Tuesday evening. I suggested ballroom dancing. The men go fishing during the day, so the ladies deserve something fun to do in the evening. Dewey agreed to let me try it."

"Dewey Smith?"

"Yes. You remember him, don't you?"

How could he forget? Dewey had been the star forward of the basketball team, immensely popular with all the girls even though off the court his IQ was barely bigger than his sneaker size. Andrew found that he didn't much like it that Sammi Jo was in contact with the ex–basketball player. He liked it even less that this bothered him.

"How did it go?" he asked, his voice studiedly casual.

"Quite well. I've been invited to come back tomorrow night."

"You must have done a good job."

"I had to. I need the business. The bank expects to be paid back." When Andrew looked startled, she asked, "What?"

"I always thought the Crawfords were well-off."

"They are."

"Wouldn't it have been easier and cheaper to ask your father for a loan?"

"Absolutely not! I mean, he offered to set up my dance studio when he couldn't talk me out of opening it, and he wouldn't have charged me interest, but there would have been hidden charges that would have cost me dearly. I like being on my own, accountable to no one but myself. It's a little scary sometimes, I admit, but not being under anyone's control is incredibly liberating. I love it."

Judging by the passion in her voice, he had struck a most vulnerable spot. Andrew had no difficulty seeing her father as controlling. Earl Owen Crawford had always been into manipulation. Had Sammi Jo married a man just like him?

Somewhat defensively she added, "I'm twenty-nine,

so I'm a little late reaching my independence, but better late than never."

"You didn't feel independent in your marriage?"

"It wasn't that kind of a marriage. I think a married woman, or any woman for that matter, is only independent if she has her own income. Or maybe is married to a most unusual man."

"You didn't work? I mean outside your home when you were married?"

"No. My working didn't fit Jonathan Ellington's idea of the perfect wife for a rising executive."

"And he wasn't 'a most unusual man,' as you put it?"

"No."

That took some adjusting and rearranging in Andrew's mind. Finally he said, "Everyone around here referred to you two as the perfect couple. The jock and the beauty queen."

She whirled around to face him, wooden spoon lifted for emphasis. Andrew blinked and involuntarily took a step back.

"For your information, I wasn't a beauty queen. That was my mother, Patricia Ann Crawford, née Henderson, as anyone who's acquainted with her can tell you in great detail."

Sammi Jo's voice had taken on a vehement tone and her face a fierce, harsh expression. He frowned. "I remember a parade or two with floats and you on one of them. Once you wore a pink gown with flowers in your hair. You were ... Miss Azalea? At the Blue Ridge Mountain Festival? The other time you held a basket of fruit and colored leaves. A harvest fest or something like that."

Sammi Jo made a dismissive gesture. "Those were

only a county thing. I took part in them because the chamber of commerce needed someone and Granddad asked me to do it. He was the mayor at the time and said something about attracting tourists and getting the business the town needed. I never went after the title of beauty queen."

The way she said the words *beauty queen* revealed that the subject held strong and unpleasant connotations for Sammi Jo. He wondered why, just as he wondered why she hadn't run for Miss North Carolina. This would have pleased her parents, and in the past, pleasing her parents had been a big thing with her. She undoubtedly would have had an excellent chance of winning the state title. Yet judging by her reaction, she hadn't wanted to compete.

Odd, he would have thought most women would have done almost anything for a shot at such a title. But then, Sammi Jo wasn't most women. Whenever he thought he had her figured out, she did or said something unexpected. Hadn't she, against all expectation, agreed to go to the prom with him, making him walk on air, and then unexpectedly left him standing on her parents' porch, ill at ease in the rented tuxedo, flowers clutched in his sweaty hand, feeling like the biggest fool in Christendom? He must not forget that.

Andrew watched her stir the sauce, cover it, and adjust the heat. Then she picked up an apple-shaped cookie jar and two small plates that matched the gold-rimmed china cups and carried them to the table. She fetched the coffeepot and her cup before she sat down with a relieved sigh. From where he stood he could see her slip her feet out of the white sandals she wore and place them on the floor with a blissful expression on her face.

"Feet tired?" he asked.

She nodded. "An occupational hazard."

"I bet the cool brick floor feels good on your bare feet."

"Heavenly. I've always loved this floor."

When Sammi Jo realized that he had seen her barefoot, she quickly slipped her feet back into the sandals.

"Sorry," she said.

"Why apologize? This is your home. If you want to go barefoot, do it."

"My mother would call going barefoot in the presence of company poor white-trash behavior. Except when she was down by the lake, I don't remember her ever going barefoot."

"She wasn't a dancer. Her feet were probably never as tired as yours."

"True, but even if they had been, she wouldn't have taken her shoes off in front of a guest. And especially not if the guest was a man and a judge to boot."

Andrew grinned at her. "Why not think of me as someone who's known you since middle school. Do you remember Mrs. Knox's class?"

"The teacher who taught us to count in Spanish with a Southern accent?"

"The very same. Weren't you surprised the first time you heard a native speaker of Spanish?"

"Surprised is hardly the right word. I barely understood a single word they said." Sammi Jo smiled until she remembered that she'd first heard the authentic language on her honeymoon in Acapulco. She had entered her marriage with such great expectations and joyous hopes. Her life should have been perfect. How could it all have gone so wrong?

Undoubtedly expecting her married life to be perfect

had been a big mistake. But she had been raised by women who passionately believed that a woman's destiny was marriage to a man who took care of her in a relationship with clearly defined roles. Independence and self-actualization were not part of a wife's role. Feminist ideals hadn't entered Sammi Jo's consciousness until she'd been married for a couple of years. In retrospect she realized how carefully she'd been protected from them all her life.

"Sammi Jo? Are you all right?"

"Sure. Would you like a cookie?" She lifted the lid off the jar.

"What kind are they?"

"Oatmeal-raisin-carob."

"Carob?" Andrew pulled his outstretched hand back. "What's carob?"

"Are you basically distrustful or just not an adventurous eater?"

Andrew quirked an eyebrow at her. "I *have* ventured beyond turnip greens and grits, but—"

"But you're not into tofu and carob."

"Maybe it's time I was." Andrew took the cookie and manfully bit into it. He chewed thoughtfully and ate the entire cookie before he rendered his judgment. "It tastes a little like chocolate chip. Not bad." He reached for another cookie.

Sammi Jo refilled his cup, repressing a smile when he took his third cookie. For cookies he'd pronounced as only "not bad," he sure seemed to enjoy them. Remembering what her grandfather had said about him being considered a catch, she wondered if women brought casseroles and cakes to his place. She couldn't keep herself from asking, "Who does your cooking?"

"I do. Well, sort of."

"What does 'sort of' mean?"

"It means that nothing I cook smells as good as that sauce simmering on your stove. It means mostly I fix frozen dinners, though on weekends when I have time I like to fire up the grill. If I say so myself, I'm pretty good at cookouts." Andrew shot her a quick look. "Next time I catch a mess of fish, you and Nate will have to come to my place. He can eat grilled fish, can't he?" Andrew watched her expression carefully.

"Yes. Fish is good for him."

"Then will you come?"

"Sure, if Nate feels up to it."

Her response had been spontaneous and natural. She hadn't felt forced or compelled to agree to come. Andrew felt jubilant. Only now he realized that another rejection by Sammi Jo would have hurt a lot. Surely that would change after he'd been around her for a while. His reaction had to be rooted in that disastrous rejection years ago when his adolescent self-esteem had been practically nonexistent. Then Sammi Jo had seemed as unreachable as the farthest star.

Now he was well-off, successful, and respected, so why had he still been worried she'd turn him down? And why would it still matter if she did? He didn't have to prove anything to anyone. Even though he wasn't movie-star handsome—and he had no illusions about his looks—he had no trouble finding dates.

"Speaking of my grandfather, here's the van bringing him back. Excuse me, please," she said and went to open the back door.

She watched her grandfather roll himself up the ramp and into the house. He stopped the wheelchair in front of her.

"Hi, Sugar. Is Andrew still waiting?"

"Yes, he is."

"Did you keep him company as I asked?"

"Of course. Did you think I'd make him wait on the front porch?"

"No. You've been raised better than that."

Sammi Jo followed her grandfather into the kitchen where he greeted Andrew warmly.

A minute or so later, Nate said, "Well then, let's get to our game. I've thought of a couple of moves that will surprise you."

"Not so fast," Sammi Jo said, planting herself in front of the wheelchair. "Dr. Williams told me he was going to come to the physical therapy session to discuss some new exercises. What did he say?"

Nate sighed. "What he always says. For me to be patient and do my exercises."

"That's all?"

"What else did you expect? You're the one who always corners the man and asks him questions."

"If you came clean and told me everything, I wouldn't have to corner Dr. Williams." Turning to Andrew she said, "Granddad never mentioned a thing about a special diet when I moved in. I found out by accident what he can and cannot eat and do. Do you know that he was brazenly smoking a cigar every evening until I casually mentioned this to Dr. Williams who nearly had a fit?"

"I was only finishing a few Cuban cigars I'd received as a gift. Throwing them out seemed like a deadly sin. I was going to quit after they were gone."

"Yeah, right." Sammi Jo snorted in a most unladylike manner. Addressing Andrew she said, "If you believe that, I have some moon rocks I'll sell you cheaply."

"And to think that she used to be such a sweet, respectful girl." Nate shook his head, but there was an affectionate gleam in his eyes as he looked at his daughter's daughter.

Sammi Jo kissed her grandfather's cheek. "You poor man. Don't you feel sorry for him, Andy Rafe?"

"We should all be treated this bad," Andrew said with a grin.

"I'll bring you some iced tea," Sammi Jo called after the men as they left the kitchen.

Andrew discovered he had trouble concentrating on his moves, knowing that Sammy Jo was just down the hall. When she joined them, carrying a tray with the promised iced tea, he noted that she had changed into exercise clothes and his already poor concentration was shot to pieces. Who would have thought that work-out clothes could look that sexy?

"You teaching another aerobics class, Sugar?" Nate asked.

She nodded. "Monday evenings it's the ladies from St. Peter's Church." Sammi Jo set down the tall glasses decorated with a slice of lemon and a sprig of mint, as well as a plate of cookies. "Granddad, you can have two of these. The rest are for Andy Rafe."

"What are they?" Nate asked, peering at them suspiciously.

"Plaster of Paris," Sammi Jo said matter of factly.

Nate looked startled for a moment. Then he grinned sheepishly. "You must admit that you've fed me some peculiar stuff. Some of which I'd never heard of, much less tasted."

"Hasn't killed you yet, has it?" She grinned back at him. "Seriously," she said, looking at Andy Rafe, "these are meringue kisses. That's egg whites and sugar with a hint of lemon beaten together and dropped on top of half a walnut. No cholesterol."

Andrew took a meringue kiss which melted in his mouth. Almost as sweet as one of Sammi Jo's kisses. That was only a supposition, of course. He'd never kissed her. Yet. "They are delicious," he murmured.

"Thank you." She smiled at him before she left.

Andrew was still thinking about that smile when he made his next move—a move that caused Nate to chortle gleefully and rub his hands in anticipation of a speedy victory.

Chapter Three

"I've always thought that nobody can cuss as charmingly and creatively as a Southern lady."

Sammi Jo gasped. "Andy Rafe, you scared me half to death. I didn't hear you come in. What are you doing here?" Sammi Jo broke eye contact and looked at the thumb she'd hit with the hammer while fixing the banister on the studio's staircase.

"When you weren't home yet after we finished our chess games, Nate asked me to stop by the studio and check on you. He was worried."

"He shouldn't have been. And it wasn't necessary for you to stop by. My grandfather worries too much."

"He has reason to worry. This isn't exactly the best neighborhood."

"It's not that bad, and I have an alarm system."

"So why didn't it go off when I walked in?" Andrew challenged.

"Oops." She shrugged. When she saw his fierce frown and his narrowed, hazel-eyed gaze focused on her she said, her tone defensive, "I guess I forgot to set it after the last class left."

36

"Don't you 'oops' me. Anybody could have walked in through that door: a drunk, a burglar, a rapist, a murderer. That's how crimes happen. I can't believe you're that careless! Don't you ever leave that door unlocked again."

"Andy Rafe, you're not my father or my husband, so don't tell me what to do. And don't take that scolding, superior tone with me. I'm not twelve years old!"

"Exactly. You're a beautiful young woman in a place not too far from a couple of seedy taverns. The low-life rednecks who drink there would think that a woman alone at night is asking for their attention. And their attention wouldn't be respectful or nice, to put it mildly."

Sammi Jo opened her mouth to argue and then closed it. Andy Rafe had a point. She had been careless. Grudgingly she admitted, "You're right. In the future I'll set the alarm."

"And don't stay here so late by yourself."

She glanced at her watch. "I didn't realize it was eleven already. I just thought I'd do a little work around here before I went home." She glanced at her thumb again.

"Let me see that thumb," he said, sitting down beside her.

"It's nothing."

Ignoring her protest, he grabbed her hand and looked at the thumb. "Doesn't look too bad, but put some ice on it anyway."

"After I fix this bannister."

"Here, let me."

"Absolutely not. I've got to learn to do stuff like this." Sammi Jo put her hand holding the hammer behind her back, out of his reach.

For an instant Andrew was tempted to try to take it from her, but, seeing the determined gleam in her eyes he decided that tact was the better policy. She wasn't ready for any physical contact with him. Not yet. Maybe not ever, but he wasn't ready to concede that point yet.

"Let me hold the banister for you," he offered. "It would be hard even for a master carpenter to hold the railing and the nail as well as drive it into the paneling."

Sammi Jo hesitated for a second before she said, "Oh, all right. Hold it right here."

"Sure you don't want me to use that hammer?"

"Why? Does pounding that gavel of yours make you an expert with the hammer?"

"No, Smartie. But I helped build my house."

"Really?" Sammi Jo looked at him with interest. "Then can I ask you for advice on how to fix things? Just advice. I want to do the actual repairs myself."

"Aren't you carrying this independence thing a little far?"

"No." Sammi Jo hammered the nail into the paneled wall. "For example, my lazy landlord promised to fix this stair railing, among other things, when I rented the place. Has he shown up to fix any of the items he promised to repair? Has he returned any of my phone calls? Heck no. I have to learn to rely on myself. Lots less aggravating and lots less expensive."

Andrew took the hammer from her and held out his hand to help her up. It felt good to hold her hand, even briefly.

"Who's your landlord?" he asked.

"Mr. Manning."

Stunned, Andrew almost dropped the hammer. It

took him a beat to recover his composure. As casually as he could, he asked, "Did you say Manning?"

"Yes."

"Which Manning?" Andrew asked.

"There's more than one?"

"Unfortunately, there's a whole clan of them," he said, his voice grim.

"I don't like the way you said that. You know them professionally? They've been in your courtroom?"

"More than once."

Sammi Jo gulped. "What did they do?"

"It's more a question of what haven't they done. Which Manning is your landlord?"

"Burl Manning."

A low grunt was the only answer Andrew allowed himself to give.

"That growl didn't sound reassuring. You know him?"

"Yes. He's probably the smartest, trickiest, and wiliest of the whole worthless bunch."

"Oh, great! Just another example of my crummy luck. This means he'll probably never come to make the repairs." She took a deep breath. "That also means it's up to me. I hope you can show me how to change a washer in a faucet."

"I can. And there are ways of forcing landlords to make promised repairs."

"How?"

"Threaten them with legal action. Take your lease and a list of the promised repairs to your lawyer—"

"A list of repairs?" she asked, her voice discouraged.

"You did get his promises in writing, didn't you?"

"Well, no. He seemed so sincere—"

"Sincere?" Andrew almost choked on the word. "Burl doesn't know the meaning of the word." He shook his head. "He must have put on quite an act. He's slick enough to be convincing."

"He was Mr. Sincerity himself." Sammi Jo sighed. "This means I'll have to change locks, get windows unstuck—what?" she asked when he emitted one of those undefinable male noises. "Don't say it, Andy Rafe," she warned, seeing his expression. "I can't afford to hire someone to do these things, so I have to do them myself. I also know I have to learn to be less trusting."

"With people like the Mannings you do. They lie even when they don't have to lie. You've got to find a different dance studio."

"What? Do you know how long it took me to find this place? And how much work I've put into making it fit for human habitation? No way I'm moving. Besides, it's not as if Pine Springs had an abundance of suitable places."

It took all of Andrew's willpower to keep himself from getting into an argument with Sammi Jo. It would be counter-productive to do so until he had some leads on a different location for her. No way was she staying in a building owned by the Mannings. Forcing himself to seem at ease, he said, "Okay. Where's that faucet?"

"I didn't mean we have to fix it now. It's getting very late."

"You got the new washer?"

"Yes."

"It won't take long to fix the faucet. Lead the way, Sammi Jo."

She preceded him up the stairs, giving him a great

view of her latex-clad hips and legs. She had the typical narrow-hipped, taut body of a dancer. Yet there was just enough roundness to her figure to tempt a man. At the top of the stairs Andrew stopped and looked around.

"So that's what a dance studio looks like," he said.

"More or less. This one is real plain, but it had the one thing I absolutely needed: a large area with a good wooden floor. I added the mirrors on the wall so the dancers can check their posture."

"What's that curtained-off area?"

"Dressing rooms. Some of the ladies in the aerobic classes like to change here. That's another thing Mr. Manning promised to do: put in a wall to turn the area into proper dressing rooms." Sammi Jo sighed. "I'm sure he'll never do that. Not when he can't be bothered to fix minor things."

"The floor is beautiful. Was it in this good a condition when you moved in?"

"Hardly. I ripped up the linoleum somebody had placed over the wood and scrubbed until my fingers bled and then sanded it."

"What's on the ground floor?"

"I'm not sure. Mr. Manning never answered when I asked him that, but I think it's some sort of storage area."

Andrew's expression hardened again. "I wonder what he owns that needs to be housed in a such a large storage area," he muttered to himself.

"The only times I've ever seen anybody enter the place has been late at night. Each time it was a large van. The kind used to make deliveries."

"How long did they stay?"

"A little less than an hour. It arrived just as I was

starting my last class and left as we began our deep relaxation. That's why I heard it. If the van had left while we were doing aerobics, I probably wouldn't have heard it over the music." Sammi Jo studied his face carefully. "You suspect the people in the van of doing something they shouldn't be doing, don't you?" Her face lit up. Eagerly she asked, "Should I keep my eyes open to see what they're up to?"

"Definitely and emphatically not! Sammi Jo, you stay away from the Mannings. Among other things, they've had a feud going with the Whittakers. I don't want you caught in the cross fire."

"A feud? As in *Romeo and Juliet?*"

"Not nearly as romantic." Andrew placed his hands on her shoulders and squeezed them for emphasis. "I mean it. Don't get involved. These are not nice people. You hear me?"

"I hear you."

He wasn't sure he could believe her. She might be well intentioned, but her curiosity might get the better of her. The idea of any of the pig-eyed, weasel-faced, women-beating Mannings being within touching distance of her chilled is blood. He'd better find her a different studio fast.

"What?" she asked.

"Nothing. I was just thinking. Now, where's the faucet?"

"Over here in the bathroom."

Though Andrew could have finished the job in half the time, he respected Sammi Jo's wish to learn. He explained the procedure and watched her do it. The pleased expression and the grateful smile she lavished on him when she successfully replaced the washer more than made up for the time lost.

Andrew walked her to her car and waited until she drove off. He looked around the area and scowled. Her dance studio was in a high-crime part of town, a fact that made him as uneasy as the identity of her landlord. Tomorrow he'd give the sheriff a call. From now on, a black-and-white unit would slowly and conspicuously cruise past the studio a couple of times each evening.

Sammi Jo clapped her hands to get the attention of the seven couples assembled in the empty clubroom of the Star Lake Resort. "Ladies and gentlemen, let's begin. Last week we covered some basics. Today we'll learn the fox-trot."

"Why the fox-trot?" the perky redhead wanted to know.

"Because it's sort of the standard of the social dances. It can be danced to a fast, a medium, and a slow beat. So once you master the fox-trot, you'll never again spend a lot of time sitting on the sidelines at a wedding or a party. Ready?"

She noted that the women seemed a lot more eager than the men, so she decided to start with the males.

"Gentlemen, please line up in a row. I'll teach you your steps first. Remember what I told you last week? The man always moves forward and the woman moves back. The man starts with his left foot, the woman with her right. That way nobody should step on anybody's toes."

"Ha! You don't know my husband," the redhead said with a grin.

"After tonight he won't step on your toes again," Sammi Jo promised. "The beat or the timing of the fox-trot is slow, slow, quick, quick, slow, slow, quick,

quick, and so on." She demonstrated. "Until you're totally comfortable, and that won't happen until you've practiced quite a lot, I want you to whisper 'slow, slow, quick, quick' as you dance."

There were some embarrassed noises from the male ranks, but Sammi Jo ignored them. She demonstrated the basic step to them, saying, "You move your left foot forward, your right foot forward, your left foot to the side and slightly forward, and your right foot closes to the left foot. Now do this and say, 'slow, slow, quick, quick.' "

She led them through these steps half a dozen times before she turned to the ladies. "As you probably guessed, your steps are the same, just reversed. Now let's chant the beat and do this."

Then both groups practiced this, with Sammi Jo going down the line and correcting and praising their efforts.

"Now we're ready to try this together." She smiled at them encouragingly.

Sammi Jo walked around to check everyone's position, making small adjustments when necessary.

"I'm going to turn on the tape, and I want everyone to chant the beat as we practice the steps."

Andrew heard the music and bid his dinner companions good-bye. He followed the dance tune to the club room. When Sammi Jo saw him, she looked surprised but didn't seem angry. She nodded to him in greeting. Andrew sat at a table in the corner and watched her teach.

Sammi Jo worked hard. She took the time to stop each couple and gently, diplomatically, demonstrated how the dance should be done. She danced with the female students, taking the lead and showed them how to follow. She danced with the male students and showed them how to lead.

And she looked great. Her golden, shimmering hair fell in waves to her shoulders which were bare except for the thin straps of her blue dress that had little yellow flowers printed on it. Low cut, but not immodestly so, it hugged her torso to her waist. The skirt was full and swirled gracefully around her long legs each time she executed a turn.

Judging from the reaction of her students, she was a good teacher. Maybe he could improve his pitiful skills on the dance floor. Even the redhead's husband seemed to be catching on, and Andrew didn't think he could be any clumsier than that guy.

An idea occurred to him. He wondered how she would react to it. Sammi Jo might shoot it down, but there was no harm in asking. Maybe after the class he could invite her for a drink. Or a bite to eat. After all the exercise she got, she might be ready for one of the resort's fabled desserts. Andrew leaned back, smiling to himself.

Sammi Jo dismissed the class after urging the students to take a couple of practice turns around the living room each evening until they felt completely comfortable doing the fox-trot. After they'd left, she collected her boom box and sat down to change her shoes.

Andrew joined her.

"What are you doing here?" she asked.

"I had dinner with a couple of judges from Asheville. The resort is famous for its food." He hoped she wouldn't remember that she had told him she'd be there. Watching her slip her feet into sandals he asked, "Your feet hurt?"

"Not too much. I'm changing shoes because I never wear my dancing shoes anywhere but the dance floor. At two hundred dollars a pair, they have to last a while."

"I had no idea they cost that much. Wouldn't you be more comfortable wearing lower-heeled shoes to teach in?"

Sammi Jo smiled. "Sure, but it's one of those un-breakable dancing conventions that the teacher wears high-heeled shoes. Have you ever watched a dance competition on television?"

Andrew shook his head. "I didn't even know there were such things."

"What sheltered lives you judges lead," she said, her voice teasing. "Anyway, the women who participate in dance contests wear heels even higher than these." Sammi Jo put her shoes into a large woven bag and stood up.

Eager to delay her departure, Andrew said, "Have you considered entering one of those dance competitions?"

"Of course. There isn't a dance teacher around who hasn't entered a contest or at least thought about entering."

"Why don't you tell me about it over a drink?" When she hesitated, he said quickly, "Or over dessert? The cheesecake here is legendary and they make their own ice cream."

"Ice cream?"

From the way she said the word, Andrew knew he had her full attention. "They have all the usual flavors, including a mocha that I can personally vouch for.

Then they have the flavor of the week made with whatever fruit is in season. Can I talk you into having a dish of ice cream with me?"

"You've hit on my weakness. Offer me ice cream and I'm putty in your hands."

"That's a good thing to remember," Andrew murmured.

"Planning to tempt me or bribe me with that information?"

"Bribe? Me?" he asked in mock consternation. "That's against the law, and I'm a judge. However, tempting isn't against the law. At least not against secular law." He wanted to tempt her with a whole lot more than just ice cream, but for right now, the dessert would have to do.

"I'll consider myself warned," she said and smiled.

Andrew stopped a waiter and asked, "Excuse me. Is it possible to sit outside and have dessert?"

"Sure thing, Judge Garroway. I'll be with you in a few minutes."

Andrew led Sammi Jo to the terrace. He heard her sharply drawn breath. "Beautiful view, isn't it?"

"Yes. I've always loved the Blue Ridge Mountains. I've never been able to decide when they look more spectacular: in the first light of day or in the last, like now. Or is that comparing apples and oranges?"

"Maybe more like comparing oranges and tangerines," Andrew said.

They seated themselves at a table at the edge of the terrace. Before them the mountains, back lit by the last light of day, appeared like undulating dark waves. Soon they were only dark shadows against the darker night.

"You want to stay out here or go inside?" he asked.

"Stay out here. Maybe the waiter will light the candle," Sammi Jo said, indicating the hurricane lamp on the table.

Without waiting for the waiter, Andrew lifted the glass dome and lit the candle with a match.

"How lovely," she murmured.

"Yes, it is." *And so are you.* Alarmed, he wondered if he had said this out loud. From her calm face, he knew he hadn't. Thank heaven.

The waiter arrived and recited the list of ice-cream flavors the resort offered. Sammi Jo settled on Heavenly Raspberry while Andrew ordered the mocha special.

After the waiter left, she asked, "What's the mocha special?"

"Mocha ice cream with chocolate sauce."

Sammi Jo smiled. "Looks like I'm not the only one with a weakness."

"You going to bribe me?" he asked.

"Bribing is against the law, but as you reminded me, tempting is not. I'll keep your weakness in mind."

Adopting a broad Southern accent, he said, "I have to warn you, little lady. Us judges are made of stern, strong stuff. We don't tempt easily." What a liar he was. Where Sammi Jo was concerned, he definitely could be tempted. Maybe even bribed. He hoped he wouldn't be put to the test.

"I have no trouble believing that you're incorruptible. I like that."

"I'm glad you like one thing about me."

"Fishing for compliments, Your Honor?"

"That's a leading question and you're overruled."

"Are you pulling rank on me? Have you sat on that

bench so long that passing judgment has become a habit?"

Though her voice was teasing, he thought he perceived a serious tone underneath the banter. He quickly reassured her. "If I thought I acted judgmental outside my courtroom, I'd resign."

"Then what would you do?"

"I was an attorney with Legal Aid before I switched over to the prosecutor's office. I could do either job again."

"Which would you rather do? Defend or prosecute?"

"I honestly don't know. Deciding that would be hard. But let's not talk about my career options. Tell me about dance competitions."

Conversation stopped while the waiter served the ice cream. Andrew waited and watched as Sammi Jo tasted hers.

She closed her eyes and savored the cold, sweet concoction. "I don't know exactly what the nectar of the gods was, but I bet it wasn't any better than this. It couldn't have been."

"I'm glad you like it. I want you to taste mine."

Sammi Jo took a sip of water to clear her palate.

"You can use your spoon," he assured her when she hesitated.

She took a taste and uttered a small moan of pleasure. "Next time I need a chocolate fix, I know where to come. I've never tasted anything with chocolate in it that was better than this."

"Do you need a chocolate fix often?"

"Only when I get very down and blue."

"A woman like you, what could get you down? Aside from Mr. Manning and his broken promises?"

What Andrew really wanted to know was if Sammi Jo was still hung up on her ex-husband.

She put down her spoon. "A woman like me? What does that mean?"

"Sammi Jo, surely you know how beautiful you are. People look at you wherever you go."

"Calling me beautiful means nothing to me. It's not a compliment. I did nothing to *earn* my looks. They're just a fortunate or unfortunate combination of genes."

"That may be true, but why does being called beautiful upset you?"

"Because it's all that ever mattered to my parents. Especially to my mother." She paused briefly. "Let's not talk about the past. This is too lovely an evening." She picked up her spoon again. "And this ice cream is too delicious to let melt."

"All right." Andrew didn't push. He had caught a glimpse of deep pain in Sammi Jo's eyes.

"You asked about dance competitions," she said, determined to change the subject. "They're held on all levels: local, state, regional, national, and international."

Andrew only half-listened to Sammi Jo's words, still trying to interpret her reaction to his comments about her looks. Had he been as shallow as everyone else and looked only at her appearance? As a teenager he probably had, but then he had been at the mercy of hormones. Now as a mature man, he had no excuse for being that superficial. Except he didn't think he had really only looked at her appearance. He was genuinely interested in what made her tick, in the essence behind the beautiful exterior. Reassured, Andrew gave her his full attention.

"Why is it so hard to find the good dance partner necessary to enter a competition?" he asked.

"Because other qualities are necessary besides technical skills. Qualities like respect, like consideration, like being treated as an equal. The partner I had in Atlanta was really good. He was versatile. He could dance traditional and classical as well as Latin dances."

"But?" Andrew prompted.

"But since he had more experience than I had, he thought he should make all decisions without consulting me. Everything had to go his way. That's not my idea of a partnership. I no longer respond well to being ordered around."

"How well I know that," Andrew said feelingly. That got a smile out of her.

"At least you were a judge in a courtroom, and it's your job to issue orders, so to speak."

"Does that mean you're no longer angry with me for doubling your community service?"

"I wouldn't go so far as to say that."

She had spoken those words in a serious tone, but Andrew could have sworn he saw a smile in her lovely eyes.

"Don't worry, Andy Rafe. I don't hold grudges. At least not for long."

"That's good to hear."

"Dancing is a happy, joyous activity and anybody who loves to dance can't stay angry for long. Or if they do, it shows in their performance."

"It does? How?" he asked.

"It's hard to explain, but I think it robs the dancing of spontaneity, of freedom. It weighs the dancer down. Keeps her or him from soaring to the music."

"Interesting," Andrew murmured. "The things I'm learning about dancers."

"Well, here's one more thing you need to learn: dancers need lots of sleep."

"A hint that you want to go home? I'll walk you to your car." Andrew placed some bills on the table and insisted on carrying Sammi Jo's boom box and her large bag. It was a little bit like carrying her school-books, something he'd never done.

After placing her things in her car, Sammi Jo turned to him. "Thanks for the ice cream and for helping me at the studio. And for listening to me go on and on about dancing."

"No thanks are necessary. I enjoyed the evening."

"So did I."

Before he realized what she was up to, Sammi Jo kissed his cheek. Then she slid behind the wheel and drove off.

Andrew stood there for quite a while, feeling the pressure of her warm lips on his skin. At that moment he felt as if he could soar higher than any dancer had ever dreamed of doing.

Chapter Four

Sammi Jo circled the courthouse twice before she found a place to park.

She had carefully avoided Andy Rafe since the night she had impulsively kissed him. It had only been a friendly kiss on the cheek, and though she had assured herself of that repeatedly, it had troubled her enough to stay out of his way. Now she could avoid him no more. It was time for her first community service report.

Maybe he would be busy in court and she could leave the report with his secretary. Sammi Jo applied lip gloss before she squared her shoulders and entered the building.

Maybe Andy Rafe had forgotten that kiss. Or maybe it hadn't meant a thing to him, and he wouldn't mention it.

Five minutes later the secretary showed her into the judge's chambers. One look told her that Andy Rafe hadn't forgotten the kiss. Sammi Jo wanted to bolt. As if sensing this, he politely pointed to a leather chair.

"Have a seat, Sammi Jo."

"Here's the report," she said, placing the sheet of paper on his desk. "I know how busy you are, so I'll just leave. What I've done so far is in the report."

"Sammy Jo, sit down. I have a ten-minute recess."

Suddenly ten minutes seemed like a long time, but she had no choice. Wearing his black robe, Andy Rafe looked serious, austere, and unapproachable. Sammi Jo sat on the edge of the chair, her sneaker-clad feet firmly pressed to the floor.

Andrew picked up the report, pretending to read it. Though he hadn't stared at Sammi Jo, no detail of her appearance had escaped him. The night at the resort she had looked elegant and glamorous. This morning, wearing jeans over her exercise clothes, her hair pulled back into a ponytail, her face free of makeup, she looked fresh, and younger than her twenty-nine years. It wasn't fair that she could look so good no matter what. He resented that. What he resented even more was the fact that he found her appealing whether she wore makeup or not, whether she was dressed to the nines or wore faded jeans. Or nothing at all. Whoa. Heat rushed through his body. He loosened his tightly knotted tie. This was hardly the time or the place to think of Sammi Jo without her clothes on.

Becoming aware of the lengthy silence, he asked, "Are you on your way to an aerobics session?"

"Yes. At the Oakwood Retirement Village." Seeing his raised eyebrow, she added, "You'd be surprised what a good workout I get leading those senior citizens."

"You never cease to surprise me."

"Sometimes I surprise myself," she murmured. Realizing he'd heard her, and judging by the gleam in his hazel eyes, Sammi Jo knew he was thinking of her impulsive kiss. His gaze focused on her mouth and lingered there. She fought the urge to lick her lips which suddenly felt dry and tingly. Actually, she felt sort of tingly all over. Was it possible that Andy Rafe was affecting her like this? He couldn't be. She simply had been dateless so long that any appreciative male look made her remember that she was a woman. That was it.

"You *did* kiss me on the cheek," he said.

Startled, she met his gaze. Lifting her chin despite the warmth that suffused her face, she said, "I wouldn't read too much into that kiss. It was an impulse."

"Are you a recidivist?"

"A what?"

"A repeat offender," he explained.

"You mean, am I going to be impulsive again?"

"Are you?" Andrew asked, his voice soft.

"Don't count on it. I'm trying to break myself of being impulsive."

"Some habits are good and shouldn't be broken," he said, his tone mock-virtuous with a slight edge.

"Do you say that to all your recidivists in court?"

"Hardly. Their repeat offenses are criminal. A little spontaneity, on the other hand, is a good thing."

"Ha! And what do you know about spontaneity? I bet you've never done a spontaneous thing in your entire life. Or given in to an impulse."

"I wouldn't be so sure of that," Andrew cautioned. What would she say if he confessed the impulse that tempted him just then? What if he kissed every inch of that angelic face of hers? Kissed her breathless until their fantasies had been sated? Well, at least his fantasies. What hers were he didn't yet know.

"What?" he asked when he became aware of her silent scrutiny.

"I'm trying to envision you being impulsive. The best image I can come up with is seeing you maybe making a reckless move in a chess game with my grandfather."

"I was thinking more of reckless moves with his granddaughter."

Sammi Jo's blue eyes widened.

Finally he'd gotten her full attention. Maybe he shouldn't continually curb his attraction where she was concerned. Maybe he should be more assertive. As he rounded his desk, a knock on the door stopped him.

"It's time, Judge," a male voice announced.

How could ten minutes be over so quickly? "I'll be there in a couple of minutes."

Sammi Jo rose and moved behind the chair. Something in Andy Rafe's demeanor alarmed her on a strictly female level. Maybe excited was a better word. "About the report? Is it what you had in mind?" she asked. A little nervous, she continued, "This reminds me of school. The way we used to ask how long a report had to be, what—"

"The report's just fine. What are you planning to do with the kids on Saturday?"

Andy Rafe was all business now. Maybe she'd misread his earlier reaction, had misunderstood his words. She felt a little let down.

"As I expected, they weren't terribly keen on participating in ballroom dancing. Since they know practically nothing about it, I thought I'd show them a video of a national competition. I'm hoping that'll make them a little more eager to learn. Also, I'll let them vote on the first dance they want to learn. You know, give them ownership of the program." She shrugged.

"Sounds like a good plan."

"Then that's what I'll do," Sammi Jo said, rushing to the door. She felt as if she were escaping rather than exiting with dignity, but she didn't care. "See you in two weeks."

Andrew walked to the window. Parting the blinds, he watched Sammi Jo walk rapidly to her car and drive away.

"Two weeks? I don't think so," he murmured. A plan was forming in his mind. Remembering that brief instant of awareness in her eyes, he smiled. Maybe just maybe she was beginning to see him, Andrew Raiford Garroway, the man, not the awkward adolescent he had been, or the solemn judge she had met in court.

As soon as Sammi Jo entered the studio, she knew something was wrong. The air felt too humid, too warm. Great. The ancient air conditioner was probably on the verge of expiring again. She sighed. She couldn't teach dancing in a hot studio, but she also doubted that she had enough money in her checking account to pay for the repairman's after-hour visit and several quarts of coolant.

Well, she had wanted to make it on her own, live from paycheck to paycheck like the vast majority of people. She still did, but it surely was a challenge to her ability to juggle payments.

When she stepped on something that crunched under the soles of her boots, she jumped back, startled. Glass.

"What on earth?" she mumbled. A few steps ahead lay a brick. A quick look at the nearest window confirmed her suspicion. Someone had heaved that brick through her window. Why would anyone do that? Sammi Jo shook her head. Since when had teenagers needed a reason to do anything?

Muttering under her breath, she swept up the glass. Then to be sure that she hadn't missed even the tiniest splinters, she moistened sheets of newspaper and wiped them over the area, a remedy for broken glass she had learned from her grandmother.

She needed something to cover the window. Not only to keep the studio cool, but to protect the precious wooden floor from the rain the weatherman had promised they'd get during the night. There had to be something in the storage shed out back that she could use. It took two trips to drag enough assorted pieces of plywood and planks to cover the window. She had just hammered the last piece into place when her students began to arrive.

"Good golly! What happened here?" George asked.

Sammi Jo told them about the brick.

"What are you going to do?" George asked in his best school principal's voice.

"I've phoned my landlord, but as usual, he doesn't answer his phone. I'd send him a letter, threatening him with legal action, but I don't have his address."

"What's his name?" Bailey asked.

Sammi Jo told him.

"I know where Burl Manning lives," Bailey said. "I don't remember the number on the mailbox since I delivered mail there only once when the regular guy was out sick. But you can't miss the house. It's on a dirt lane, halfway up Blackberry Road. Know where that is?"

Sammi Jo thought for a moment before she nodded. "The road that circles Balsam Rock."

"That's the one."

"Why can't I miss the house?" she asked.

"Because it's the only place that's got more old cars and parts of cars lying around it than Riley's Junkyard," Bailey said. "All the other houses in that area have been bought and fixed up by city people who wanted a place with a view."

Sammi Jo thanked him and started the class.

Three hours later, after getting groceries, she impulsively pointed her car north toward Balsam Rock. The air felt hot and heavy, the way it did before a summer storm. It wasn't until she reached Blackberry Road that she noticed how strong the wind had become. Its force rocked her compact car, but she was too close to her destination to turn back.

She spied the rusting hulks of cars before she saw the low, white house crouching behind them. Lights filtered out through the windows at the front of the house. Someone was home.

Places in the country were usually guarded by a dog or two. No sooner had she cautiously opened the door then two dogs rushed towards her, barking furiously. When their loud barks roused no one in the house, Sammi Jo knew she had to do something. She had driven this far and no way was she leaving without seeing her landlord. Her gaze fell on the grocery bags in the backseat.

Did dogs eat fish? Even if they did, she wasn't

about to feed them red snapper at six dollars a pound. Rummaging through the bags, she located a package of turkey franks. She tossed two franks as far from the car as she could. The dogs found them, devoured them, and came back for more, their tails wagging. They looked expectantly at her.

"You're hungry, huh?" They whined. Sammi Jo flung more franks at them before she stepped out of the car.

She heard a screen door slam and watched a man approach. While the barking of the dogs hadn't aroused anyone's interest, their silence had. Despite the fading light, she knew the man walking toward her wasn't Burl Manning.

"What do you want?" he asked, his tone surly. "Git," he yelled at the dogs. He picked up a stick and threw it at them. "Worthless critters."

Sammi Jo wanted to tell him that if he fed the bone-thin animals, they'd be better watchdogs, but she restrained herself. He didn't look like the type who took constructive criticism well.

"I came to see Mr. Manning," she said.

"I'm Mr. Manning."

"I meant Mr. Burl Manning."

"Pa ain't here," he snapped.

"Who are you?"

"Junior Manning. What do you want with Pa?"

"I'd like for him to make the repairs at the studio he promised to make."

Junior took a step closer. "You're that dance lady." He squinted at her through the dim light. "Pa didn't tell me how pretty you was."

Sammi Jo didn't like his leering expression. As

calmly as she could, she asked, "When can I speak to your father?"

Junior snickered. "That's hard to say. He ain't gonna be around for a spell."

Junior took another step toward her. Sammi Jo forced herself to stand her ground though his strong smell, a combination of old sweat and stale beer, hit her hard. She tried to take shallow breaths.

"Maybe I can help you. What needs fixin'?"

"For starters, the window someone tossed a brick through tonight."

"What? Them damn Whittakers! I'll fix them but good. Shiftless snuff chewers."

Sammi Jo thought this a classic case of the kettle calling the pot black, but kept this opinion to herself. When Junior paced back and forth, furiously venting his agitation, she slid behind the wheel and fastened her seat belt.

"Tell your father that I expect him to make the promised repairs." Without waiting for a reply, she shifted into reverse and backed the car out of the driveway.

She hadn't driven ten feet when a lightning bolt split the dying light, followed instantly by a clap of thunder that made her flinch. And then the rain came. It didn't start gently, but fell in impenetrable sheets that rendered visibility next to zero. She wanted to stop, but the dirt road was too narrow for her to pull over safely. She'd have to wait until she reached Blackberry Road.

As Sammi Jo turned onto the paved street, her tires hit something slick. The car spun around and plunged into the ditch. When her heartbeat returned to near normal, she took stock of her situation. There was no way she could get out of the ditch by herself. She would have to call a tow truck. Her cell phone was in the big woven bag which she had tossed into the trunk before going to the grocery store.

Sammi Jo would have uttered a number of phrases that might even have shocked Junior if she hadn't been deeply grateful for having escaped injury. Getting wet while retrieving her cell phone was a small enough price to pay.

Tall weeds impeded her steps. By the time she had inched her way to the trunk, the rain had plastered her blouse to her body. Despite the fact that her vision was hindered by the rain, she saw the headlights of a car sweep past. Moments later she thought she heard a car door slam. In the next lightning flash she saw a tall figure slide down into the ditch. The beam of a powerful flashlight trapped her. She raised her hand to shield her eyes.

"Sammi Jo? I don't believe this. It *is* you."

That voice could only belong to one man.

"What the heck are you doing here?" Andrew shouted over the sound of the rain and the wind.

"What am I doing here? I thought I'd make a lei-surely rest stop." That man could ask the most irritating questions. She flicked the rain from her face. "What are *you* doing here?"

"I was on my way home when I saw your head-lights."

"Can you pull my car out of the ditch?"

Andrew shone the flashlight over the car and the surrounding area. "Even though the ditch is shallow, it's going to take a tow truck to pull you out."

"I was afraid of that."

"Come on. I'll take you to my house."

"That's not necessary. I can call from here. My cell phone is in the trunk," she said.

"If you think I'm going to let you sit alone in this ditch for heaven only knows how long, the rain has softened your brains. How did you end up in this ditch anyway? Driving too fast?"

"No. There was something slick on the road. Oil, maybe."

"Or dirt and loose gravel washed onto the macadam."

Andrew opened her car door, removed her purse, and switched off the headlights. The slam of the door sounded angry.

"Let's go."

Sammi Jo didn't move. He was ordering her around as if she were a recalcitrant four-year-old.

Andrew turned. "What's the matter now? Are you coming? I don't enjoy getting soaked."

"Then why did you stop? I didn't ask you to."

"I thought I ought to be a Good Samaritan."

"If I recall correctly, the Bible doesn't say anything about the Good Samaritan being such a grouch. Go on. I don't need your help."

"Not much you don't," Andrew muttered. He reached for her arm. The wet leaves caused Sammi Jo to slip. He caught her before she fell. For a moment she leaned heavily against him before she pulled back.

"Sammi Jo, I'm sorry I snapped at you, but it's been a long, frustrating day. I'm wet, tired, and hungry. Aren't you?"

"Yes," she conceded in a reluctant tone.

"Okay, then. Will you please do me the honor of coming to my house to wait for the tow truck?" he asked with exaggerated patience and courtesy.

"Yes. And thank you for stopping."

Unexpectedly, he chuckled. "What's so funny?" she demanded.

"Us. We're the only two people I know who'd stand around in a major rainstorm to argue about who waits where."

"That's because of your legal training. Lawyers are confrontational."

"True, but I'm no longer a lawyer."

"Old habits die hard, Your Honor."

Andrew chuckled again. "Come on. Though we hardly need to hurry. We can't get any wetter than we already are."

He kept his arm around her waist to help her up the rain-slick embankment.

"I'll get your seat wet," she said when he opened the passenger door.

"It's vinyl and it'll dry. Hop in."

From his four-wheel-drive vehicle Andrew phoned the service station he customarily used. After telling them the location of her car, he did a double take.

"I was going to ask what you were doing out here, but now I don't need to. Burl Manning lives on that dirt road. You went to see him, didn't you?"

"If you already know that, why do you have to ask?"

Andrew slammed his palm against the steering wheel. "Didn't I ask you to stay away from the Mannings?"

"And didn't I tell you that I'm through being ordered around by men?"

"I didn't order you around."

"It sure sounded that way to me."

"I only warned you about the Mannings for your own good," Andrew claimed.

Sammi Jo groaned. "Every time someone does something for my own good, it isn't."

"Can't you accept help without getting your hackles up?"

"I can if that's what it really is."

"What else could it be?" Andrew asked with a frown.

"Control and manipulation."

Startled, Andrew took his eyes off the road for a moment to look at her. The car swerved.

Sammi Jo gasped.

"Sorry," Andrew said, touching her arm in a reassuring manner. "I swear I'm not trying to control or manipulate you."

"Good. Then we'll get along a lot better."

She didn't sound as if she believed him. Her ex-husband and her father had done a real number on her. It would take a while before she believed or trusted him. He had patience and he would make time.

"Why did you go to the Manning place?"

"Because Burl never answers his phone. I'm beginning to suspect that he gave me the number of some obscure pay phone that no one ever picks up."

"Did anything happen that you needed to see him about?"

"Somebody threw a brick through one of the studio windows. Junior thinks it was the Whittakers."

"Damn. The feud might heat up again. Just what we need," Andrew said, his tone disgusted.

"Junior said his father wasn't going to be around for a spell. Would they feud without the head of the family?"

"They might if Burl gives the order."

"Junior didn't say how long his father would be unavailable."

"Seven months and four days."

Sammi Jo turned to face Andy Rafe and asked, "How do you know that?"

"Because Burl violated his parole, and now he has to serve the rest of his sentence."

"Oh, great. Now I'll never get anything repaired." She sank back in the seat, discouraged, then sighed deeply.

"What if I help you? I mean, show you how to fix things," he added hastily. "I told you I did some hands-on work when my house was built. I learned a lot in the process." Sammi Jo remained silent. "Sammi Jo? Did you hear my offer?"

"Yes, thank you. Looks like I won't have much choice but to ask for your help."

She wasn't eager to ask for his help, but after the first time or two, it would be easier for her. At least he hoped so. Andrew turned down a side road and then into his driveway. In the garage he said, "I'll make some coffee. It won't be as good as yours, unless you volunteer to make it?"

Sammi Jo stepped out of the car. Her full skirt hung soddenly, heavily around her legs. Even as she stood there, a small puddle was forming at her feet. "Andy Rafe, I can't go into your new house. I'll ruin your floors."

Andrew braced his hands on his hips and regarded her through narrowed eyes. "You can come into my house on your own two feet, or I can carry you. No way am I letting you stand here dripping wet until the tow truck gets your car. The mechanic said he wouldn't take the truck out until the rain lets up. Looks like that'll be quite a while."

Her tailored, Western-style blouse clung to her. Andrew swallowed hard. How could he be angry with her for her stubbornness and be attracted to her at the same time?

Sammi Jo bent down, grabbed a handful of the hem of her skirt and blotted her face. Since the skirt was dripping wet, this didn't help much.

Hoping he had his voice under control, Andrew said, "What if I bring you a towel and a robe and then we can put your clothes in the dryer? Okay?"

She nodded. "And a newspaper to put my boots on."

When Andrew returned, he handed her a towel. She wrapped it around her hair, turban style. He watched her lean against the wall to take off her boots.

"What's with the Western look? I thought you taught ballroom dancing."

"I do, but this couples' group from my grandfather's church asked me to teach them line dancing. I'm no expert in Western dancing, but they only wanted to learn a few simple steps, and dancing is dancing." She held out her hand. "Well?"

"Oh yeah." Andrew hoped he hadn't been staring too obviously at her. Quickly he handed her the robe and a plastic laundry basket. "I'm going to change my clothes too. Just come on in when you're ready."

Sammi Jo nodded. As soon as Andy Rafe entered his house, she took off her wet clothes. All but her panties. Though they were damp, she couldn't bring herself to take them off. The robe, navy with white piping on the collar and the cuffs, felt soft around her body. A trace of the expensive-smelling scent he wore lingered in the fabric. Holding the collar against her face, she inhaled deeply, and her mood lifted. She combed her hair, rubbed lip gloss over her mouth, and padded barefoot into the hall which led to the kitchen.

"Wow," she said reverently. She walked wide-eyed around the central island.

Andy Rafe returned, buttoning a short-sleeved shirt. He watched her. "You like my kitchen?"

"It's a dream kitchen. And you don't even cook!"

He shrugged. "I told the architect I wanted the best."

"I think you got it. There's even a baking center with a marble board for rolling out dough." She trailed her fingers admiring over the smooth, cool surface.

"Any time you want to bake, feel free to come over." He picked up the laundry basket and headed for the utility room.

When he returned he said, "I'm curious. What's that white net thing that looks sort of like a skirt?"

"A crinoline. Makes the skirt swirl nicely when dancing."

"Oh. The things women wear," he said wonderingly.

"Do you mind?" Sammi Jo asked, gesturing toward the wall of cabinets.

"Be my guest."

Opening doors and pulling out drawers, she oohed and aahed over the contents and the arrangements.

"Sammi Jo, come here please. Which of these frozen dinners do you want?"

She placed the back of her hand dramatically over her forehead. "The man has a state-of-the-art kitchen, and he also has every frozen dinner available in western North Carolina. Is that schizophrenic or what?" Pointing her finger emphatically at the freezer she said, "Please close the door on that pitiful sight. I think I can find enough ingredients to fix us a simple but real meal. Unless you'll suffer withdrawal symptoms if you don't get your nightly ration of frozen food?"

"Very funny." Andrew grinned back at her. "Go for it. What can I do to help?"

"Look in your refrigerator and tell me what you find."

Andrew hunkered down and stared into the vast, white, and mostly empty space. He'd been meaning to go to the store. "There's orange juice. Milk. Bread. Cheese. Beer. Lettuce."

"Lettuce is good."

"There are some tomatoes."

"Even better. Please take those out. For better flavor, you shouldn't store tomatoes in the fridge. Any sign of an onion?"

"Do green onions count?"

"Definitely." Sammi Jo rummaged through the pantry. "A bag of pasta. Olive oil. What's this? Will wonders never cease? A Bulgarian garlic pot. And there's even some garlic in it! We're ready to rumba."

Andrew smiled at her enthusiasm. "What else can I do?"

"Wash the lettuce, please. What kind is it?"

Andrew looked puzzled. "There are different kinds?" He held up the head of lettuce for her to see.

"Iceberg. I was afraid of that. It's the blandest of all the lettuces. Next time buy lettuce with dark green leaves. Better taste and lots more nutritional value."

"You're good for me, Sammi Jo. I'm learning a lot from you."

"What's the phrase you legal eagles use? Quid pro quo? You're teaching me how to fix things, and I'm teaching you how to take better care of yourself." She flicked him a long, assessing glance. This was the first time she'd seen him wear jeans since their high school years. He looked good in them.

"You don't want to end up looking like a lot of guys in their thirties: flaccid muscles, poor posture, beer belly, and rolls around their middle. Very unhealthy."

Andrew squared his shoulders. "I work out."

"I thought you probably did. It shows. You look fit, and fit is sexy."

He nearly dropped the head of lettuce. Good thing Sammi Jo hadn't asked him to chop something. He might have cut off a finger. As he washed the lettuce, he watched her surreptitiously. At least he hoped he wasn't being too obvious.

His robe was yards too big on her. Though she had belted and bloused it, it almost reached her ankles. He watched her elegant feet move across the floor. Did she enjoy the cool feel of the ceramic tiles?

"Andy Rafe, why don't you use the salad spinner?"

His eyes darted over the various items on the counter.

Sammi Jo opened a cabinet and removed a white plastic bowl. "This is a salad spinner. You place the washed lettuce in here like this and then spin the bowl. It removes the water so the dressing can cling better to the leaves."

Andrew tried it. With a grin he gave it a couple more spins.

"Having fun?" she asked.

"Yeah, I am."

He seemed a little surprised by the discovery.

When the bowl stopped spinning he said, "I think there's a bottle of dressing in the pantry."

"Bite your tongue. We have olive oil and red wine

vinegar. We'll make our own. We sure don't need all those chemicals the commercial dressing contains. Not to mention the strong, unnatural taste."

Every time she moved her right arm, the robe slipped off her left shoulder. Andrew felt himself gripped with the intense desire to scatter kisses along her delicate collar-bone. Who'd have thought that a bone could be such a powerful turn-on? Luckily for him, Sammi Jo moved to the stove and out of his reach. If he'd made a move on her, she might have run out into the rain and walked all the way home. On the other hand, she might not have. He'd have to—

"Andy Rafe, who equipped your kitchen?"

"An interior decorator. I confess I have no idea what some of the gadgets and small appliances are that he put on the shelves."

"What a shame to let this beautiful kitchen sit un-used. And you eating frozen dinners."

He watched her shake her head as if deeply pained. "You could teach me how to cook," he suggested.

"Cooking takes time, which is something neither one of us has a lot of."

"I meant it when I said that you could come over any time you felt like baking something. That goes for cooking too. Let me know when, and I'll give you a key so you can get in."

"Do you always give out the key to your house that readily?"

"No. You're the only one I've offered it to."

Sammi Jo paused in the act of stirring the penne to look at him. Then resuming her task, she said, "Letting myself in wouldn't be a good idea. What if you were entertaining a woman?"

"I don't bring women here."

Sammi Jo grappled with this unexpected statement. Finally she said, "I'm sorry you felt compelled to bring me here. I didn't mean to invade your privacy and your refuge."

"What are you talking about? I practically dragged you in here, so how was I compelled?

"By your chivalry. You felt you couldn't leave me stranded."

Andrew realized she wasn't ready to admit to herself that for her he had made an exception. Somehow the idea threatened her. "Sammi Jo, how much have you dated since your divorce?"

"How much?" She shrugged. "Some." She poured the pasta into the colander. "How about you? How much do you date? According to Mrs. Pruitt, you're a most sought-after man." Andrew laughed, but it wasn't a happy sound. He didn't answer her question.

She tossed the pasta with the sautéed vegetables and carried the dish to the breakfast bar where Andy Rafe had set two plates. She dressed the lettuce and divided it into two bowls.

After they'd eaten the pasta, which Andy Rafe pronounced excellent, and were sipping their coffee, she asked, "How come you're not married?"

He raised an eyebrow at her.

"Hey, you asked me some personal questions. Fair's fair."

"Okay." Andrew thought for a moment. "I don't know." When he saw her skeptical expression, he elaborated. "When I was young, I didn't have time. Between studying and designing computer programs to support myself, there weren't any hours left in which to pursue women seriously. Then after law school, I had to establish myself in my career."

"Other men do all that and still manage to pursue women and get married. Or is that the problem? You don't want to do the pursuing but want to be pursued instead?"

"Are you offering to do the pursuing?"

Sammi Jo ignored the warm glint in his hazel eyes. "We weren't talking about me, and you haven't answered my question."

"Why I haven't married?"

"That's the one."

With her lovely eyes watching him seriously, expectantly, he knew she deserved an answer. "I guess I haven't met a woman who made me feel compelled to rush into matrimony."

"What would compel you?"

Andrew shrugged. "The feeling that I couldn't do anything else *but* marry her."

"Most people call that love."

"I suppose so," he admitted.

"Why are men so afraid of that word?"

"Love doesn't scare you?"

"Marrying for something less scares me even more," she replied.

"Is that what happened to you?"

She was silent for so long that Andrew didn't think she would answer.

"Looking back with a cool, detached mind, I wonder. I thought at the time that I loved Jonathan and maybe I was even in love, but I never felt the kind of compulsion you talked about. What I felt wasn't that intense. Maybe that was part of the reason the marriage didn't last."

She looked troubled. Andrew sensed there was more

to the story. Softly he asked, "Looking back with sober detachment, why did you really marry him?"

"As I said, I thought I loved him." She thought for a moment. "But also because my parents were constantly on my case to compete for the Miss North Carolina beauty contest," she blurted out.

Andrew didn't understand the implication of her statement immediately. When he did, he said, "Once married, you couldn't compete."

She nodded.

"And?" he continued.

"You must have been one heck of a prosecutor. You don't stop, do you?"

"The truth is usually made up of layers. I like to peel back the layers to get at the essence."

Sammi Jo studied his face. With a slight nod acknowledging the truth of his statement, she continued. "Do you have any idea what it's like to take part in such a competition? You have to parade in front of a bunch of people, knowing that they're saying things like, 'Her hips are too big. Her bust is too small. She isn't pretty enough. She has no talent.' Makes you feel like a piece of merchandise. Like some soulless object. And for what? So my mother could vicariously relive her moment of glory? So my father could use the title for publicity for his business? No!"

Sammi Jo carried her plate to the sink. She turned the water on full blast.

She was clearly agitated. Too agitated. Andrew knew she had told him only part of the truth. The easy part. But he also realized that she wasn't ready to reveal the layers lying near the core. He carried his plate to her.

"I have a dishwasher," he said.

"I know, but there are only a few dishes. We can do these by hand."

He guessed that the mechanical act of washing dishes soothed her. He picked up the dishtowel and dried them.

The telephone rang. Andrew answered it. "That was the service station. Their tow truck just left the garage."

"Perfect timing," Sammi Jo said.

Andrew didn't think so. Though he had never invited any of his dates to his house, he liked having Sammi Jo there. Somehow she didn't seem like an intrusion. Granted, they argued. Granted, his dates usually put themselves out to be sweet and agreeable while Sammi Jo did not. Not only did she not bother with the "I'm on my best dating behavior" game, she didn't disguise the challenging, peppery, vinegary side of her nature. And yet he preferred her company to any other woman's he'd ever met. Go figure.

Chapter Five

Two nights later, when Sammi Jo left the studio, she found Junior Manning and a companion waiting for her in the parking lot. With a pang of alarm, she assessed the situation. There was no one else around. She had meant to leave with her students, but straightening up the place had taken longer than she had anticipated. Nothing for her to do but brave it out.

"Good evening, Mr. Manning," she said, her voice coolly polite, her manner regal.

Junior lifted a finger to the greasy baseball cap on his head. "Evenin'. I been waitin' for you."

"Really? Let me guess. You talked to your father and he sent you to tell me that he's ready to fix all the items he promised to repair. That's wonderful."

Junior's mouth dropped open. He blinked. He shifted from foot to foot. "Well, no. Not exactly."

He placed his foot on the fender of her car in an attempt to appear nonchalant. Sammi Jo took a quick look at the other man. Somewhat shorter but with the same squat, no-neck build, he bore a startling resemblance to Junior. Another member of the Manning clan.

Junior cleared his throat. "I came to tell you that you gotta move out of the studio."

"What? You must be kidding. I have a signed lease for a whole year."

"Well, I'm unsignin' it."

His companion chuckled as if this were the wittiest thing he'd ever heard. Sammi Jo directed a long, icy look at him which silenced him. He spat a stream of tobacco juice on the ground. She shuddered in revulsion.

"You can't 'unsign' it because you didn't sign it in the first place," she informed Junior.

"Oh yeah? Says who I can't unsign it?"

"Says the law. Only your father can break the lease and that not without penalties."

"Well, Pa ain't here, and I'm takin' over his business dealings. You gotta get out."

"I don't think so. Check with your lawyer. Given your family's encounters with the law, I'm sure you have one."

Junior took his booted foot off the fender and hitched up his pants which had slid below his beer belly.

"Go get her, Junior," his companion urged with a cackle.

"Shut up, Ray."

Junior continued toward Sammi Jo. He stopped two steps in front of her. "I don't have to check with my lawyer. The buildin' belongs to us, and I'm tellin' you to get out. We need the space."

"So do I. When you read the lease, you'll find that it's binding. Breaking it isn't as simple as you think it is. If you don't want to consult a lawyer, ask your father."

Junior hitched up his pants again. "Pa ain't here, and I'm takin' over."

This sounded like a power struggle within the family. Maybe this dissension would work in her favor. "Does your father know about you wanting to break the lease? Why don't I get in touch with him and ask what he wants."

"Now you listen here—" Junior broke off when the headlights of a car swept over him. In a flash he and Ray retreated to their pickup and moments later gunned it out into the street.

The black-and-white patrol car made a slow sweep through the parking lot and waited while Sammi Jo got into her car and drove off.

Odd, lately every evening she had noticed the patrol car driving through the parking lot about the time she was ready to leave. Almost like a black-and-white angel watching over her. The notion made her smile.

Halfway home she noticed that the streets were dark and that the traffic lights weren't functioning. The storm that had swept through earlier must have put the power out in this part of town. Alarm surged through her. Was her grandfather all right? Sammi Jo stepped hard on the gas pedal. If she got a speeding ticket, so be it.

At first glance the house looked dark. Then she caught a glimmer of light. It seemed to come from the porch. Granddad must have lit some candles.

"Granddad?"

"We're out here. It's too hot in the house with the air-conditioning off."

We? Who was visiting him? She hadn't taken the time to look at the cars parked in the street. She rushed onto the porch.

Andy Rafe rose. "Good evening, Sammi Jo," he said.

What was that man doing here? It wasn't a Monday evening. She inclined her head in greeting. Then she bent down to kiss her grandfather on the cheek.

"How long has the power been out?" she asked, fanning herself. Even out on the porch the air was close and sweltering.

"A couple of hours. The storm knocked out a transformer. We probably won't have any power until early morning. Andrew stopped by to see if I needed anything."

"That was nice of him."

Though she'd kept her voice friendly, the look she gave him was not. Andrew merely smiled at her. He was fairly certain that she would have enjoyed kicking him in the shin just then.

"Andrew stayed to keep me company. He opened the windows to get some air into the house, but it hasn't helped any. There isn't so much as a whisper of a breeze. We may have another storm before the night's over," Nate said.

Andrew added, "We decided to play a few hands of gin rummy, and so far your grandfather is winning."

As if on cue, Nate said, "Gin." He placed his cards on the wicker table. "Want to join us, Sugar?"

"No thanks. It's too hot. I'm going to change my clothes and make us some lemonade."

Andrew watched the material of her full skirt swirl as she turned. She was wearing high-heeled shoes, so she must have taught a dancing class. Her wide belt with a rhinestone buckle emphasized her small waist. She was perfectly proportioned. He couldn't think of anything that needed to be changed or improved. Of course, he was hardly objective, he admitted to himself ruefully. Thinking about Sammi Jo made him lose the next two games.

She returned with three glasses of lemonade. He did a double take when he saw that she had changed into a swimsuit.

"After I drink this lemonade, I'm going down to the lake for a swim. Granddad, you want to come with me? Remember how much you enjoyed it the last time we went?"

"Yeah. In the water I'm not nearly as clumsy with my leg as I am on land. Almost makes me feel the way I used to feel before the stroke. You want to come with us, Andrew?"

"I'd love to go for a swim," Andrew said, not bothering to disguise his eagerness. "Especially since I'm losing almost every game."

"Well, you know what they say about that, don't you? Unlucky at cards, lucky in love," Nate said.

"Hope you're right," Andrew muttered fervently. He cast Sammi Jo a sideways look. Mistake number one, he told himself, as heat rushed through him. The yellow one-piece suit she was wearing was modest, and yet it struck him as the sexiest garment he'd ever seen. Risking a quick glance at her legs, he knew that was mistake number two. She had the most gorgeous legs he'd ever seen: long, shapely, toned to perfection. What he wouldn't give to hold her. Sweat broke out on his forehead. Could he get any hotter without bursting into flames? He heard Nate speak to him as if from very far away. Using his considerable willpower, he forced himself to listen.

"I'm sure you can find a pair of swim trunks in the chest on the back porch that'll fit you," Nate said. "The water will cool us off. I feel the heat the way I never used to. In my old age, my blood must have gotten thin."

"Since you're taking medication for just that purpose, I sure hope your blood is thin," Sammi Jo said with a smile. "Besides, thin blood is supposed to make you feel cold, not hot."

"Now you tell me."

She handed each of the men a flashlight. "I'll wash these glasses and wait in the kitchen for you."

Sammi Jo lit the hurricane lantern they kept in the kitchen. Though its light was meager, she could clearly see Andy Rafe when he joined her, wearing a pair of the borrowed swim trunks. What she saw made her catch her breath.

"You weren't kidding when you said you worked out," she finally said. She couldn't keep herself from staring at his wide shoulders, his flat stomach, his trim waist. And his legs looked like the legs any male dancer would give his eyeeteeth for.

"I'm using one of the bedrooms in my house as an exercise room. I'll show it to you next time you come. Since you're more knowledgeable about physical fitness, maybe you can give me some pointers on what I need to add."

"I'd be glad to."

They lapsed into a tense silence. They were suddenly shy around each other. Sammi Jo glanced at him quickly, furtively, when she thought he wasn't looking at her. He seemed to be doing the same thing. She felt enormous relief when her grandfather wheeled himself into the hall and called out to them that he was ready.

Sammi Jo walked ahead with the lantern to light the path for her grandfather. Andrew brought up the rear, carrying their towels. Intermittently, the moon broke through the cloud cover, casting a silver sheen over everything.

Andrew watched the gentle sway of of Sammi Jo's hips. Hers was not the practiced walk of a woman deliberately setting out to snare a man's attention. He almost wished it were because it would mean that she was interested in something other than making the dance studio a success. Not that he really wanted her to notice all men or even a few men—just him. And Sammi Jo had done that during those few magical moments in the kitchen.

All he had to do now was build on that awareness. But subtly. Anything obvious or clumsy and he would spook her. She would look for ways to avoid him. She was good at that. Carefully he rehearsed the invitation before he uttered it.

"I'm planning to go fishing on Saturday morning. Would you two do me the honor of joining me for supper Saturday night?" Andrew asked. "I'll grill Saturday's catch. You can't get fish any fresher than that."

"Will you listen to the man's confidence! What if you don't catch anything?" Sammi Jo challenged.

"I usually do. If not, the marina owner employs several guys to fish for him. I'll buy what I need from him."

Though he was too far away for her to see his face clearly, Sammi Jo thought she'd heard a smile in his voice.

"I'd love some fresh fish," Nate said, "but Sammi Jo, isn't this the Saturday you're driving to Asheville to meet Greg?"

"Oh, yeah, it is," Sammi Jo said.

Who was this Greg she was driving all the way to Asheville to see? Andrew could have kicked himself for not asking her out sooner. Sammi Jo was a beautiful woman. Probably every guy she met made a move on her. And here he'd thought it best to move slowly. He couldn't believe it.

"I can't cancel this meeting," she said, "but can we have a rain check on the fish supper?"

"Sure." Part of him admired her for not wanting to cancel a date when another opportunity presented itself, and part of him was disappointed and let down.

"After Saturday's session, are you going to decide if Greg will be the one?" Nate asked.

The one? What did that mean? Fear raced through Andrew and settled on his chest like a crushing, heavy weight. When had she had time to get so serious about this Greg? Unless he was someone she'd known in Atlanta.

"Granddad, keep your fingers crossed that this one will work out. I'd hate to start the search all over again."

The search? For a husband?

"Sugar, I'm keeping my fingers crossed. The alternative doesn't please me at all. I'd worry something fierce if you had to drive to Charlotte and back late at night."

"I've pretty much ruled out driving to Charlotte. For one thing, it's too far, and for another, he's too opinionated and too full of himself to make a good partner."

Partner? A dance partner! Of course. She'd fleetingly mentioned needing a new partner. The relief that surged through Andrew almost made him tremble.

"Greg's awfully young. I don't know how reliable he'll be. On the other hand, his body is in great shape and at peak performance," Sammi Jo said.

"I'd sure like it if Greg could occasionally drive to Pine Springs and you could practice here," Nate said. "You doing all the driving doesn't seem fair."

"As soon as Greg sees the studio, I'm sure he'll be willing to alternate places. We only get a small section of the Asheville studio when we rehearse there. Here, we'd have the whole place to ourselves," Sammi Jo said.

"In that case, invite him to take a look, Sugar."

"If I can persuade his girlfriend to ride along, I'm sure he'd be even more willing to come to my studio. Granddad, could I take the small television that's upstairs to the studio? She could watch while we rehearse. I'd offer to bring her books, but she didn't strike me as a reader."

"The set's upstairs for you to watch. If you won't miss it, Sugar, I sure won't."

Greg had a girlfriend. How absolutely wonderful! Andrew felt like jumping high into the air and clicking his heels like Fred Astaire. He resisted the temptation to try this, fearing he would land on his butt and make a fool of himself.

"This Greg, is he any good as a dancer?" Andrew asked.

Sammi Jo made a so-so motion with her hand. "He has potential. Good potential. As I said, he's young and inexperienced. But that isn't all bad. For one thing, he doesn't have to unlearn a whole lot of poor techniques. And he has loads of energy and enthusiasm."

"What kind of ballroom dancing does he prefer?" Andrew asked.

"Unfortunately, he's really into swing and jive and I prefer the Latin dances, but I'm sure we can work out a compromise."

"Doesn't a competition ask you to demonstrate all forms?" Nate asked.

"Yes, but we can choose one, and since one of the required categories is swing, I think I can persuade Greg to pick the samba or the rumba."

They arrived at the small wooden pier that jutted out into the lake.

"Do you need help getting into the water?" Andrew asked Nate.

"No. Getting in is easy. I just sort of take a shallow dive. The water is deep enough for that. Getting out, though, I need a little help. Surprisingly, Sammi Jo was able to help haul me out."

"Why surprisingly?" she asked, a serious expression on her face.

"Don't get riled up, Sugar, but to look at you, there isn't much meat there. I guess what there is must be all muscle."

"You better believe it," Sammi Jo said, flexing her arm muscles playfully.

Andrew said, "Let me see you do that again." When Sammi Jo flexed her muscles, he ran his hand over her arm. "Very impressive." Her skin felt silky and warm, her arm taut and firm. He let his fingers linger a moment longer than was necessary.

Sammi Jo turned to her grandfather and helped him stand on his good leg. He bent forward and plunged into the water. She waited until he surfaced and was holding onto the steps with his strong arm. Then she slid into the water.

Andrew joined them. "Hey, this is great. I wouldn't have thought that the water would be this cool."

"You two can swim out to the platform. I'll hang onto the steps and practice my kicks. This way I'll get in a little more exercise and surprise my therapist, the slave driver."

"Granddad, be fair. She's an excellent therapist and only pushes you for your own good. Yell if you need help or want to get out."

"I may never get out. I feel so good in the water. Go on. I'll be just fine."

"Race you to the platform?" Andrew suggested.

"Such reckless confidence," she said. Without warning she added, "You're on," and struck out toward the platform.

Andrew overtook her, but she soon caught up with him. Her crawl stroke looked deceptively easy and leisurely, but he soon discovered that she was a strong, steady swimmer. He had to concentrate to stay even with her. They reached the platform simultaneously.

"We tied. Or maybe I got here a fraction of a second before you," he claimed.

"In your dreams, Andy Rafe. I set the all-time record, reaching this platform."

"Oh, yeah. You used to invite your crowd out here. I heard rumors that you skinny-dipped."

"Not on this platform! You must be thinking of the one at the other end of the lake. I wouldn't have dared to do any skinny-dipping here, not with my grandfather around. When I had friends over it was always during the day. Remember the big tree halfway between the house and the lake?" When Andrew said he did, she added, "Granddad usually sat in a lawn chair under that tree. He claimed he was watching in case anybody needed help. Yeah right." After a moment she added, "Though he was a lifeguard when he was young."

Andrew had spent whole summers fantasizing about Sammi Jo swimming in the lake. Those fantasies had both delighted and tormented him. "So, did you skinny-dip at that other platform?"

"Absolutely not! Only the really fast crowd did that. I wasn't a member."

"Moral scruples?"

"Try fear," she said.

"Sometimes I think most moral scruples are rooted in fear, and that's not entirely a bad thing. What were you afraid of?"

"That my parents would ship me off to that all-girls school they threatened me with when I didn't want to do something. What were you afraid of back then?" she asked.

"That I wouldn't ever fit in anywhere. Or amount to much, given my undistinguished background." And looks, he added silently. Back then he hadn't had the money for extensive dental work to straighten his teeth or for the corrective lenses which eventually made his glasses unnecessary.

"But you were so smart! How could you have been afraid of not succeeding?"

"I wasn't afraid of not succeeding on an academic level. It was all the other levels I felt insecure about."

"I have news for you. No teenager, no matter how popular, is ever secure about everything. It goes with the territory."

"It's hard to believe that you were insecure. I used to watch you at school. You sailed through the halls as if you owned them. Like a princess about to be crowned queen."

"That's because my mother made me walk through the house with a big dictionary on my head. I didn't dare slouch."

"It was more than that, and you know it." Andrew moved closer until his hands were next to hers, holding onto the platform.

"Andy Rafe, can I ask you a professional question?"

"I know nothing about dancing," he joked.

She kicked him lightly with her leg. "You know what I mean."

He moved a little closer, his leg touching hers. He felt as if he'd been zapped by an electric current.

"You didn't answer me. Can I ask you a legal type of question?"

He had to put a little space between them if he was to think rationally. "Go ahead and ask me."

"If somebody wants to break a lease, they can't just do it, can they?"

"No. Depending on the lease, there are certain penalties. Do you want to break your lease on the studio?"

"No, no. I love the studio. Junior wants to break it."

"How do you know that?"

"He was waiting for me tonight."

"At the studio?"

"In the parking lot."

Andrew bit down on the cuss words that threatened to burst from his mouth. The idea of that cretinous Manning waiting for her in the poorly lit parking lot scared him as much as it angered him. "What exactly did he say?"

"That with his pa unavailable, he was taking over the family business. He claimed he needed the space."

"What for?"

"I have no idea. Just as I have no idea what the family business is."

"Officially, it's fixing up old cars, but I'm willing to bet the First Amendment that their income from that wouldn't be enough to keep them in chewing tobacco. Fixing up cars entails too much hard work. None of them is exactly fond of hard work."

"Then how do they live?"

"That's a good question. I suspect they run some stills deep in the woods on the other side of the mountain. That's what got Burl arrested. I wouldn't put it past them. Unfortunately, the sheriff hasn't been able to find all the stills nor catch the other Mannings tending them. He doesn't have the manpower to search that many hundreds of acres of forest or put permanent surveillance on the large Manning clan."

"You don't suppose he'd want to use the studio to house a still? What exactly do you need for a still?"

"Water and a source of power, corn, and sugar, I think. But I can't believe that even Junior would be dumb enough to try making moonshine right here in town."

"What else could he want the studio for?"

"I don't know. Ask your lawyer to look at your lease and advise you what to do." Andrew hesitated. He knew his next suggestion might upset her. "All in all, it wouldn't be a bad idea to keep your eyes open for another location. Not having to deal with the Mannings would be worth the move."

Sammi Jo shook her head. "I don't have time to look. In addition to earning a living, I also need to work on the dance routines with Greg if we want to enter the competition this fall. And I definitely want to enter a competition. Also, I don't think there's another location that would be nearly as suitable. And Burl did rent the studio to me. I'm not moving, and that's final."

He heard the rock-hard determination in her voice. She wasn't going to move unless she was forced to.

"Maybe I can help you find another place."

"Andy Rafe, you have enough on your plate. This is my problem. I'll handle it."

Why did she have to be so set on doing everything herself? He'd have to find a way to help her without her knowing it.

"Let's swim back," she suggested.

"Not yet." Andrew touched her shoulder to make her turn to face him. She was holding onto the platform with one hand. He placed his hands on the platform on either side of her.

"Sammi Jo, put your hands on my shoulders and let go of the platform."

"Why?"

"Because I want to try something."

"What?"

"Something I've wondered about for over twelve years."

"What on earth could that be?" she asked.

"Just do it and trust me."

She smiled and shook her head. "Every time a man says 'trust me,' it's like a warning signal, saying that the woman should run in the opposite direction."

"Sammi Jo, do you really think I'd do anything to hurt you?"

"No. At least not deliberately." She placed one hand

on his shoulder but continued to hold onto the platform with the other. Sammi Jo felt his body move closer, almost close enough to touch hers. She saw him looking at her mouth. Her heartbeat accelerated. Her throat tightened. "What have you been wondering about?"

"What it would be like to kiss you."

"You've wondered about that since high school?" she asked, a touch of wonder in her voice. "That's crazy."

"I know. It's high time I found out the answer to that tormenting question, don't you think?" he asked gently.

She nodded. She placed her other hand on his shoulder a little tentatively. To stay afloat, she had to move closer, her body lightly touching his.

Andrew felt heat slam into him. *Easy*, he told himself. *Don't blow it now by coming on too strong.* He lowered his mouth to hers and kissed her gently, tenderly. He felt her tremble. When her lips yielded and parted slightly, he deepened the kiss. He felt her hands slide around his neck. Her scent filled his senses, the taste of her mouth, lemony and sweet at the same time, fed his hunger, the touch of her fingers burned through his skin, scorching each layer. Andrew felt his heart beat, almost painfully strong. He heard his blood roar in his ears. Just when he thought he might lose not only control but perhaps even consciousness from the power of the kiss, Sammi Jo wrenched herself away from him.

She looked at him with wide eyes, silently, wonderingly. Her lips remained parted. She breathed shallowly.

He thought he heard her murmur something like

"sizzling samba," before she dove under his arm and started to swim toward the pier.

Andrew waited several seconds, trying to bring his body under control, trying to gather enough strength to swim after her.

Chapter Six

"Sammi Jo?"

Startled, she stopped at the bottom of the stairs and turned. Andy Rafe was standing on the porch, the screen door between them. "I thought you'd left," she said, walking toward him.

"I did. I got as far as the sidewalk. I couldn't leave without speaking to you."

Sammi Jo waited for him to continue. She didn't know what made her more anxious: the thought that he would talk about the kiss, or that he wouldn't.

"Did you really think we could just walk away from each other as if nothing had happened?" he asked.

"We kissed. It's something people do all the time," she said, trying to sound casual.

"Maybe other people kiss all the time, but we don't. At least not yet," he added in a low voice. "May I come in, or do you want to come outside?"

"Neither! We better keep the screen door between us."

"Ah."

"And what is that pleased 'ah' supposed to mean?" she challenged.

"That deep down you don't consider it an ordinary kiss either. If you did, you would be willing to get close to me and maybe risk another kiss."

"You're so sure of yourself," she said, irritation coloring her voice.

"I wasn't. Not until you kissed me back."

More than anything else Sammi Jo wanted to deny this, but she couldn't. She *had* kissed him back. Had she ever! Even now, a small shiver of pleasure skittered down her spine. Irrationally, that irritated her even more. "It's very annoying when someone is right all the time," she snapped.

"Why does it upset you that you responded to my kiss?" When she didn't say anything, he added, his voice tinged with bitterness. "I see. I'm still not good enough. Is that it? I'm still that nerdy kid from the wrong part of town."

Sammi Jo jerked the screen door open so fast it made him blink. She stepped out on the porch. Facing Andy Rafe she said, her voice passionate, "You're so wrong I can't even begin to tell you how wrong you are! Why are you so hung up on what happened years ago? Or what part of town you came from? You're more successful and more respected than any of the boys who came from up the hill, so why does it still matter?"

"It matters. The past always matters. It's part of who and what we are."

"You sound just like my attorney. Isn't that a fatalistic view of life? Doesn't that imply that we can't escape our past? Or our roots? Our upbringing?"

"It's not fatalistic. We can come to terms with the

past, and if we're lucky, we can even rise above it. If not, we repress it. But whatever we do, it'll always be part of who we are."

"So in your view of life, part of me is condemned to always be that . . . what was it you called me? Golden girl?"

"Yes."

"Oh, isn't that just great," she muttered. "Why did you call me that anyway? Because of the color of my hair?"

"Partly, but mostly because your life was so golden, so perfect. At least it seemed that way to an outsider."

"That's the key word: *seemed.*"

"What was so imperfect about it?"

"How much time do you have?" she asked.

"You were the adored only daughter of—"

"Don't list all that!" Sammi Jo said rather imperiously. Then she sighed. "I know most people considered me lucky, and I suppose my life would have been nearly perfect if I had wanted the same thing my parents wanted for me. But I didn't."

"You mentioned not wanting to be in beauty contests—"

"Those awful beauty contests! They ruined everything!"

"How? I don't understand."

Sammi Jo walked to one of the big, white porch pillars and braced her arms against it. After a few seconds she spoke.

"More than anything else I wanted to take ballet lessons. I lived and breathed ballet from the time my grandparents took me to a performance in Chapel Hill. I begged and pleaded to be allowed to take lessons. I promised to be so good. To do everything my parents wanted me to do if only I could take lessons. Year after year I begged until the year I realized I was too old to start. I'd missed my chance. It was too late."

Andrew heard such utter defeat in Sammi Jo's voice that it tore at his heart. He laid his hand on her shoulder. "I don't understand. Lots of girls take ballet lessons. Why couldn't you? It wasn't as if your parents couldn't afford them."

A small, bitter laugh escaped her throat. "Because my mother feared that taking ballet would make my legs too muscular, and a girl with muscular legs would never win a beauty contest."

Andrew was too stunned to say anything. He took her into his arms and held her. When she didn't pull back, he laid his cheek against her hair.

"Maybe I wouldn't have been very good. Maybe I would never have made it out of the corps de ballet of some minor company, but I would have liked to have had the chance to try! Everyone should have a chance at their dream."

What a cruel thing to do to a little girl. No wonder Sammi Jo hated beauty contests. He thought she might be crying silently, but he knew it would be unwise to say anything. Instead he held her and stroked her hair, still damp from their swim.

After a while Sammi Jo freed herself and walked a few steps away from him. "I'm sorry. I didn't mean to dump all that on you."

"That's okay. No need to apologize."

"How did we get on the subject of the past anyway?" she demanded. "Oh yes. You accused me of thinking you weren't good enough. That that was the reason I didn't want to talk about the kiss." Sammi Jo touched the petunias trailing from the hanging pot above her. "It's not you. I can't get involved with any man right now."

"I'm very relieved to hear it isn't me, but why can't you get involved?"

"Do you have any idea how much effort it takes to make a relationship work? How much time and energy? I don't have either the time or the energy."

"I have both," Andrew said. "Why not let me do most of the work in making this relationship successful?"

She shook her head emphatically. "It takes both people. Believe me, I know. I tried to make my marriage work, but I couldn't. Not by myself."

"Is that what made your marriage break up?"

"That and the fact that Jonathan didn't want children. In retrospect, I should be glad that he didn't. He would have been an absentee father, and eventually I would have been a single mother. So I guess it worked out for the best."

Andrew was stunned. How could a man not want Sammi Jo as the mother of his children? What kind of selfish jerk had she married? Though it was too dark to see her eyes, he'd heard the pain in her voice. His heart ached for her. Sammi Jo had been rejected more cruelly than she had rejected him twelve years ago. Actually, looking back from the vantage point of maturity, he realized that she hadn't had a choice back then. Not really. Her parents' stranglehold on her had been complete and suffocating. The last weak twinges of old resentment drained from him.

"I'm sorry, Sammi Jo." He shook his head. "I can't believe there's a man who wouldn't want to be the father of your children. To me that's inconceivable."

"Thanks, but maybe you're not completely objective."

"I don't know about that. I think I see you quite clearly."

"Uh-oh. That doesn't sound good. You're going to tick off my failings one by one, aren't you?" she said, trying for a light tone.

"No. You're not perfect, but neither am I. Your shortcomings don't scare me."

"What does scare you?"

"That in your need to prove your independence you'll sacrifice what has started between us. That would be a crime, Sammi Jo. And don't say that there's nothing. Not after the kiss we shared."

"Andy Rafe, you're not listening. I don't want to be involved with anyone, but if I did, I'd certainly consider you."

"That's promising."

"Merciful macarena! You're either the biggest optimist I've ever met, or you don't hear well." Moderating her exasperation, she repeated, "I haven't the time nor the energy for a relationship, not even a casual one."

Andrew didn't want a casual relationship, but this wasn't the time to tell her that. Softly he said, "You're tired. You work too hard."

"Really?" Sammi Jo asked, her tone of voice ironic. She looked at him meaningfully.

Andrew felt his face redden. "I know the community service I assigned you is part of the reason you have to work so hard, but I can't rescind the order. It wouldn't be ethical."

"I didn't ask you to do that. It wouldn't be fair to the other demonstrators if you did."

"Thanks for understanding, Sammi Jo." Andrew ran his hand through his hair, thinking. "Can't you turn down some of the requests for private lessons? Or cancel some of the aerobic sessions you teach? I get tired just thinking about all you do."

"I can't cut back. I need the money. Even though I couldn't become a ballet dancer, I want to be involved in other forms of dancing. I have to be. It's what I want to do more than anything else. Don't you see why the studio has to succeed?"

Andrew nodded. He did understand. The question was: how could he help her? He knew better than to offer her a loan. Or suggest that she ask her parents for help. Still, he couldn't back off. He had to find a way to make her life easier, not only so that he could help her, but so that he could woo her. He'd think of something. He had to. After that first kiss, he pined— hungered—for countless more. He couldn't imagine ever getting enough kisses, just as he couldn't imagine going through life without loving this woman.

"Speaking of being tired, I'm exhausted, and tomorrow will be another long day. Good night, Andy Rafe."

"I'm not giving up on us," he told her softly, insistently.

"There's nothing there to give up on," she replied.

"Yes, there is. I'll see you soon." He rubbed his thumb over her soft mouth. "Good night, Sammi Jo," he said and walked away.

"Darn. I left the new tape in my car. I'll run down and get it. In the meantime, I want you to practice the steps we learned last time," Sammi Jo told her class. She popped the video into the machine and pressed the play button. As the strains of steel guitars filled the studio, the couples arranged themselves into a line, eyes on the video screen.

Sammi Jo rushed down the stairs. The parking lot was only dimly lit as several of the lamps were broken. If she had a responsible landlord, the lights would have been fixed long ago. She wondered if it would do any good to ask Junior. Probably not. Not when he wanted her out of the studio.

She had just removed the tape and relocked her car when the Manning van pulled up in front of the downstairs door. She watched two familiar figures emerge: Junior and his no-neck cousin. Should she confront Junior now about the lights?

Sammi Jo had decided to ask him to replace the lamps when something about the postures of the two men stopped her. They appeared to be scanning the parking lot watchfully. What were they looking for? Instinctively she remained immobile, figuring that they couldn't see her as her car was parked in one of the darkest parts of the lot. After a moment they unlocked the van and each removed what appeared to be a large object. As they passed under the light over the door, she recognized the objects as fenders from a car. There was something very familiar about those fenders. Why on earth were they lugging auto parts into the storage area? The way she remembered the Manning house, there seemed to have been enough room around it to store dozens of car parts.

Sammi Jo shrugged mentally. Who could figure out the reasoning of someone like Junior? She debated whether to make a run for it or wait until they'd finished unloading. She made her way closer to the building carefully, ducking down behind a car when she heard their voices. She waited until they had entered the building a third time, loaded down with car parts, before she sneaked back inside.

Once in the studio she dismissed all thoughts of the Mannings as she concentrated on teaching. It wasn't until she left with the last of her students that her thoughts wandered back to Junior. The van was gone. However, a sheet of notebook paper under her windshield wipers caught her eyes. She unfolded it. The note was typed or printed on a computer.

You better get out of the studio if you know what's good for you. I ain't kiddin'.

Under the writing, the author of the note had drawn a stick figure, its thin arms raised in a boxer's stance, the disproportionally huge hands balled into fists. The message was unmistakable.

Sammi Jo shuddered and looked around the parking lot quickly. She saw no one who looked like Junior. That didn't mean he couldn't be hiding nearby. As the last students left the lot, she slid behind the wheel, locked her doors, and quickly drove off.

All the way home she debated whether she should take the note to the police. But what could they do? Junior hadn't explicitly threatened her. Nor was there any proof that he had written the note, though in Sammi Jo's mind there was no doubt. Junior wasn't the brightest penny in the till, but even he undoubtedly knew not to leave his fingerprints on the note. She decided she would ask her grandfather's advice. However, when she got home, he was already asleep.

Sammi Jo checked her messages. Then she called her answering service.

"Lucinda, it's me. Anything special scheduled for me tomorrow?" she asked.

"Yup. A new client. Said he needed some refresher lessons. He's been invited to a wedding and hasn't danced in years. I told him he probably needed five lessons. Told him your fee, and he accepted without batting an eyelash. Sounded real nice too, and educated. Not one of them shiftless, worthless, gone-again Joes. You play your cards right, hon, and maybe you'll catch yourself a live one."

"Lucinda, I don't want a live one—"

"Shoot, hon, you sure don't want a dead one!"

While Lucinda laughed heartily, Sammi Jo rolled her eyes.

Still chuckling, Lucinda said, "There's a call on the other line. Gotta go. Bye, hon."

Why couldn't people believe that she really didn't want to get involved with a man? First Andy Rafe and now Lucinda. Deep down even her grandfather probably didn't think she was serious about no involvement. Sammi Jo sighed and went into the kitchen in search of food.

Unbidden, images of Andy Rafe's kitchen flashed through her mind. They'd had such a great time there, cooking and eating and talking. If anyone had told her that she would enjoy his company that much, she wouldn't have believed them. He had a way of insinuating himself into her thoughts, her feelings, her life. The man was dangerous to her independence.

And then there was the kiss. Who would have suspected that Andy Rafe would be such a terrific kisser? Or that she would respond to that kiss like a woman on the edge of emotional starvation? Sammi Jo feared that all her good intentions of resisting him might fail if he kissed her again. The best defense against that kind of temptation was to put distance between it and her.

So far she had managed to do just that. Monday night she didn't come home until she was sure the chess games had ended. Then, when her biweekly report was due, she waited at the court house until the guard closed the door to the courtroom in which Andy Rafe presided before she took it to his office and left it with his secretary. Pleased, Sammi Jo reflected that she had done well avoiding that dangerous magistrate. All she had to do was continue to stay out of his way and she should be safe.

While Sammi Jo waited for her new student, she watered the red geraniums she had planted in an antique whiskey barrel. The flowers were doing better in the light from the north window than she had hoped. They added a touch of color to the neutral-toned studio.

"Sammi Jo."

She jumped, spilling a little water on the gleaming wooden floor. "Andy Rafe! Now look what you made me do." She grabbed a handful of tissues and wiped up the water.

"Didn't you promise me you'd set the alarm last time I was here?"

"I'm expecting a student any minute, so I left the door unlocked for him."

"That's not good enough. Anybody could have walked in, even Junior Manning."

Andy Rafe was right. Briefly she debated whether she should tell him about the note, but decided if she did, he'd feel he had even more cause to scold and boss her around. She decided to ignore his reference to Junior. "What can I do for you?"

"You know the student you're expecting?"

"Yes." Sammi Jo glanced at the clock on the wall. "He's a couple of minutes late."

"No, he isn't."

Sammi Jo frowned. "What do you mean?"

"I'm the student," Andrew said, watching her reaction closely.

Though a number of conflicting emotions flitted through her, hurt pride was the strongest. Sammi Jo stood very straight. After drawing a careful breath, she said, "I know I've mentioned several times that I need to earn money, but I'm not a charity case, so turn around, Andy Rafe, and go home."

For an instant he merely stared at her, too astonished to speak. With a fierce frown he asked, "Are you refusing to teach me? If you are, I can easily make a case that I'm being discriminated against."

"What? Are you threatening legal action? I don't believe this!"

"Why did you tell me to go home? Why do you think I'm doing this only because you need money? Do you think I'm that calculating?"

"Aren't you? Do you have a legitimate reason for wanting to take private dance lessons? Or did my grandfather put you up to this since I won't take money from him?"

"Nate doesn't know I'm here. And I have a legitimate reason for being here, though I don't really need one. I might just want to improve my dancing. I have as much right to avail myself of your services as anyone else." Andrew took an envelope from his jacket pocket and handed it to her. "Read this."

Sammi Jo took the envelope. Before she removed its contents, she knew what it would be. Only wedding invitations arrived on such heavy and elegant stationery.

"I told the woman who makes your appointments that I needed to brush up on my dancing before I go to this wedding." Andrew watched the faint pink hue spread over her face. "I'm expected to dance with the bride and her bridesmaids. I'd rather not stomp on their feet if I can help it. Will you teach me?"

Sammi Jo handed him the envelope. "Since you have a good reason and since you asked so nicely, I'll teach you. I'm sorry I questioned your motives."

"When you want to, you can apologize very nicely," Andrew said with a smile. "Thanks."

"Don't thank me yet because I'm going to make you work very hard. Your feet definitely will not thank me. We have only five lessons to get you ready."

"In other words, you don't want your student to disgrace you."

"You've got that right. And you're paying me, so let's get started. I always give my students their money's worth."

"Yes, Ma'am." Andrew gave her a little salute.

Sammi Jo was all business now. She showed him the proper way to hold her, which, to his chagrin, wasn't cheek to cheek. Still, with his arm around her, her hand in his, he was a lot closer to her than he'd been for over a week. She was extraordinarily skillful in avoiding him, the minx. He had allowed her to get away with that in order to lull her into a false sense of security. Now she was his and his alone for five sessions, and if he played his cards right, for a few more after that.

"What dances do you need help with?" she asked.

"All of them," he answered quickly.

"Really?"

"Sammi Jo, I haven't danced since the last wedding I attended, which was six years ago. And I wasn't a good dancer to begin with. I've probably forgotten everything I knew about dancing."

"To some extent dancing is like riding a bicycle. You can't have forgotten *everything*." Sammi Jo reflected for a minute. "You'll probably need to practice the waltz. They usually play at least a couple of slow waltzes at a wedding. And you should know a few simple swing steps and the cha-cha."

"What about the fox-trot?" he asked, remembering that he had watched her teach it at Star Lake Resort.

"And definitely the fox-trot."

"That can be danced to a slow beat, can't it?" he asked, thinking of holding her close.

"Yes, it can." Sammi Jo popped a tape into the machine. "The fox-trot is a versatile dance, so we'll start with it in a medium tempo."

There went his hope for holding her against his heart. Still, just being with her was enough to take his breath away.

"I go forward and you move back?" he asked, liking the fact that the man was in control.

"Yes." Sammi Jo chanted the beat just loud enough for him to hear.

Andrew inhaled the scent of her hair which fell in loose waves down to her shoulders. He tried to identify the smell but couldn't. It reminded him of a warm summer's day filled with the fragrance of flowers and sun-warmed fruit. He loved the scent and breathed it in deeply.

"Andy Rafe, dancing should be fun. I can feel the tension in your shoulders. Please relax."

Fat chance of that. He hadn't been able to relax when he'd tutored her in math all those years ago, and he couldn't relax now. At least his palms weren't sweating now. Back then he had wiped his hands on his jeans before he'd rung her doorbell, and his mouth had been so dry he'd had trouble speaking to her. He had made some progress since then, but his insides were still twisted in tangly knots and his nerve ends felt raw and ragged. If he didn't want to disgrace himself and step on her toes, he'd have to concentrate strictly on the dancing. Ignore her scent, ignore the softness of her hand in his, ignore the warmth of her back which he felt through the thin, silky material of her dress. Blast, this wasn't going to be easy.

When the tape stopped, Sammi Jo said, "You're doing great. I stopped chanting the beat some minutes ago and you haven't made a single error. At this rate, you won't need five private lessons."

"Oh yes I will," Andrew said quickly. "The fox-trot has always been the easiest for me. Wait till we try the waltz. If Strauss could see me, he'd undoubtedly be sorry he ever created that dance. We'll probably need five sessions for the waltz alone. I'm not even sure you can teach it to me."

"Of course I can teach you to waltz. I've never failed to teach any of my students. Naturally, some turned out better dancers than others, but all could go out on the dance floor with a measure of confidence. Andy Rafe, I don't want to hear any more defeatist statements."

"Yes, teacher," he said with mock meekness. He

hadn't exactly lied about his ability to dance, just minimized it a little.

"We'll fox-trot now to a faster beat," she said.

"And then to a slower beat?" he asked, trying hard to mask his eagerness.

Sammi Jo nodded and stepped into his arms.

Andrew concentrated hard, too hard, and consequently it took longer to master the quick-step version of the dance. As Sammi Jo wasn't watching the clock, they got to the cheek-to-cheek part even though the session was officially over.

Well, it wasn't exactly cheek to cheek, but almost. At least when they started out. Slowly, slowly enough so that she wouldn't notice, he hoped, he drew her closer. Their bodies were almost touching as they moved in perfect harmony. When they turned, they got even closer. He felt her body grow rigid, but he wouldn't release her.

"It's your turn to relax, Sammi Jo," he murmured in her ear. "I've dreamed of dancing like this with you for years."

Incredibly, she did relax against him. Her silken hair brushed against his lips, her upper body curved into him, instantly sending electricity through him. Andrew clenched his teeth. When the music ended, he wasn't sure whether he was sorry or glad. Self-control took a lot out of a man.

Andrew watched her exchange her high-heeled pumps for a pair of sandals. He carried her boom box as they walked to the parking lot. Both stopped at the same time beside her car. What would happen if he kissed her again? She might cancel the dance lessons. He couldn't risk that.

"Granddad said that you invited us to a cookout a week from Sunday."

"I did. Nate told me that your partner is coming for a practice and that you probably won't be able to make it. Is that true?"

She nodded. "But I'll be able to pick him up so you don't have to drive both ways."

"Good. You'll probably be starved after all that dancing. Shall we save you some food?"

"That would be nice. I have to warn you though that I'm usually quite famished after practice and can put away a lot of food."

"I consider myself warned. Your appetite doesn't frighten me, Sammi Jo." She flicked him a quick look, as if she wondered if this were a double entendre. "I meant I'll cook extra," he continued, smiling.

"Oh. Well, I better get on home."

"Sammi Jo, I've been wondering. . . ." he broke off, suddenly hesitant.

"What have you been wondering?"

"If you'd go to that wedding with me? You know, give me moral support and dance with me to refresh my memory of the steps. That waltz really worries me."

"I just bet it does." Sammi Jo tried to hide a smile. He was so blatantly transparent that she couldn't get mad at him. "Why don't you just ask me to go with you?"

"Okay, I'm asking. Will you go to the wedding with me?"

"Yes."

Andrew opened his mouth and shut it. He grinned ruefully. "That simple, huh?"

"I'm a simple woman. Easy to understand."

"Yeah, simple and easy, like deciphering ancient Germanic runes."

"I don't think I like being compared to ancient runes, Germanic or otherwise," she quipped.

"So sue me."

"As if I could ever win against you!"

Good thing she didn't know how easily she could win anything and everything he had, including his heart. Heck, she'd already won it. The question was, did she want it?

"Is it an afternoon wedding? Evening? I need to know so I can dress properly."

"Evening. Six o'clock. There will be a buffet supper, followed by an evening of dancing."

"Sounds lovely."

Sammi Jo placed her bag in the car. "Why don't you put the boom box on the backseat, please."

After he did, she placed her hands lightly on his chest. Her touch hit him like a shock wave.

"Thanks for inviting Granddad for a fish supper. With me being so busy and him not able to drive, he doesn't get out much. He tries to hide it from me, but he's been depressed. I worry about him. It was really sweet of you to invite him to lunch on Sunday."

"I enjoy Nate's company. Believe me, it's surely no hardship being with him." When Sammi Jo leaned toward him, he asked, "Are you going to kiss me on the cheek again?"

"If you prefer the cheek—"

"No, not necessarily," he said hastily. His heart beating wildly, he waited and let her make the moves. Her hands slid upward until they cradled his face. Her lips met his with a sweet, gentle pressure, and for an instant he could have sworn that the ground swayed beneath his feet.

Chapter Seven

The week passed so quickly that Sammi Jo found herself in front of her closet a mere six hours before the wedding wondering what to wear. Thanks to the active social life her ex-husband had insisted on, she had several dressy outfits. After laying out half a dozen dresses on the bed, the choice came down to two. Sammi Jo carried them downstairs.

"Granddad, which one should I wear tonight?"

Nate lowered the newspaper and studied the two dresses his granddaughter was holding up. "Well, they're both beautiful. The black one is elegant, but I favor green for a wedding. Green's a hopeful color. The color of new life. Of new beginnings. That's what your grandmother always said. She was fond of green."

"Green it is." Sammi Jo turned to go back upstairs.

"Are you through working for the day?" Nate asked.

"I wish. I only came home to take a quick shower and change clothes for my community service."

"How's that going?"

111

Sammi Jo frowned thoughtfully. "Hard to tell with teenagers. They don't think it's cool to get enthusiastic about anything. On the other hand, they keep showing up. You tell me how I'm doing." She shrugged.

"Andrew said you're doing a fine job."

"That's good to know," she said, her voice dry. "You'd never know it from the comments he makes, or rather fails to make, about my reports. I sometimes wonder if he even reads them."

"He reads them."

"How do you know that?"

"Andrew told me."

"You two talk about me?"

"Of course. We're both fond of you, so from time to time, we talk about you."

Sammi Jo wasn't sure she liked being the topic of conversation, but she had no time to worry about that now. "I've got to go. I'm running late."

Leaning back against the plush upholstery, Sammi Jo sighed.

"Was that a sigh of relief, regret, resentment? What?" Andrew asked.

"Relief. The last time I sat down today was at breakfast."

"And now I'm dragging you off to an evening of dancing. Sorry about that."

"Don't be. We won't be dancing the whole time. There's the ceremony and then supper. You did say there would be food, right? I'm starving."

"There will be food. I promise." He glanced at Sammi Jo again, as he'd been doing ever since they'd left the two-lane highway and were heading toward Asheville on I-26. She looked so lovely he had trouble keeping his eyes off of her. The vibrant green color of her dress looked spectacularly good on her.

"What?" she asked. "You keep looking at me. You don't like my dress? I wish you'd said something before we left the house. I could have worn something else."

"I love your dress. It looks terrific on you. You look terrific."

"Then what?"

"I was wondering if you were wearing earrings. I can't tell with your hair down."

Now it was Sammi Jo's turn to stare. "You wondered about my earrings?" she asked, her tone incredulous. "Why?"

"I wondered what kind you'd wear with that dress. Emeralds?"

Sammi Jo laughed. "Only if I were rich. Emeralds are expensive." She paused. "Actually, I have a pair I could have worn with this dress. They're some sort of semi-precious stone. Tourmaline, maybe. I can't remember. I didn't even think about earrings." She looked at him curiously. "You have a thing for women's earrings?"

"No. You rarely wear jewelry so I was curious."

"Most of the time I'm in too much of a rush to bother with putting any on." She shrugged.

"But you don't dislike jewelry?"

"Not really, though I wouldn't sell my soul for a gem. Not even for a handful. Why are you so interested in jewelry?"

"Don't be so suspicious. I'm trying to get to know your likes and dislikes. Is that a crime?"

"You're the judge. Is it?"

Andrew chuckled. "I love your sassy mouth, Sammi Jo. In more ways than one."

"Oh?"

"I'm tempted to stop the car right now and kiss you."

"I don't think a state trooper would consider kissing a legitimate reason for stopping on the interstate. He'd give you a ticket. Judges aren't supposed to get traffic tickets, are they?"

"Might be worth it," Andrew murmured.

"*Might* be? You know beyond a shadow of a doubt that it would be worth it. You've known that from the first kiss."

"True, but this was a good try to get a few more samples. Don't you think?"

Sammi Jo rolled her eyes.

"I'm wondering about something you said a minute ago."

"What?" she asked.

"About not selling your soul for jewelry."

"Oh. That." She took a breath before she replied. "Some women will forgive a man just about anything or can be talked into doing something they'd normally never consider, provided a good piece of jewelry appears at the optimum moment. You should see my mother's jewelry box. And I'm not even talking about the pieces she keeps in the bank vault."

Andrew flicked a quick look at her, but couldn't read her expression. Not that he needed to. Her voice was tinged with bitterness and disappointment.

"No more talk about jewelry," she said firmly. "Tell me about this wedding we're going to. How do you know the groom?"

Andrew respected Sammi Jo's wish and told her

about the bride and groom. By the time he finished, they had arrived at the church. Andrew introduced her to the groom and then let an usher escort her to a seat.

Sammi Jo watched the wedding guests arrive, all in an upbeat mood. Weddings made people happy. Too bad that almost half of the marriages ended in deep unhappiness, bitterness, acrimonious confrontations, or at best, indifference. She had to throw off the dark memories, Sammi Jo told herself firmly. Though she wasn't superstitious, she wouldn't cloud the couple's happy day with negative thoughts.

She listened to the organ music, sniffed the air, fragrant with the baskets of flowers decorating the church, and nodded to the people around her until she was caught up in the festive mood.

The ceremony was lovely. The bride and groom exchanged heartfelt vows and looked at each other with deep emotion and affection. Sammi Jo thought that Andy Rafe looked distinguished in his black tuxedo. Distinguished and attractive. And masculine, and sexy. Sammi Jo's heart beat faster.

The wedding party adjourned to the ballroom of a nearby hotel. After going through the receiving line and congratulating the beaming couple, Andrew steered her toward the buffet table.

"I promised you food, and food you shall have. I'm a man who keeps his promises."

"Because you just heard some pretty serious promises being made?"

"No, because all of my training has conditioned me to think that promises, vows, and contracts must be honored, or serious consequences will be levied."

Sammi Jo nodded. "Marriage is a contract. That's what's so puzzling."

"What is? You lost me." Andrew spooned some scalloped potatoes onto Sammi Jo's plate, which was still empty except for a piece of salmon and some green beans.

"That men, who'd be scared to death of breaking a business contract, don't seem to think twice about breaking the marriage contract with the flimsiest of rationalizations. Explain that to me, Your Honor."

Andrew shrugged. "I've considered that. The only explanation I can come up with is that the penalties for breaking the marriage contract aren't financial. At least not right away."

Sammi Jo stopped, bringing the line at the food table to a dead halt. She looked at him. Then she nodded. "You're right. It's usually quite a while between the breaking of the vows and the divorce."

Andrew nudged Sammi Jo to get her to move forward. She seemed deep in thought, so he added food to her plate every time he added some to his.

Tables had been set up around the periphery of the dance floor. Andrew located one that was set for two. "Is this okay?"

"Fine," Sammi Jo said and sat down. When she looked at her plate, her eyes widened. "I don't remember getting all this food. How on earth—"

"You said you were hungry."

"Not this hungry."

"I'll take what you don't want."

Sammi Jo picked up the dinner roll and the drumstick and placed them on his plate.

"Something else I learned about you," he said. "You don't like chicken and dinner rolls."

"Yes, I do, but not when I have potatoes and salmon

on my plate already." She tasted the salmon. "Lovely," she murmured and began to eat in earnest.

When her hunger was stilled, Sammi Jo sighed contentedly. "This is very nice. Candlelight and fresh flowers on the table and the band warming up."

"That reminds me of my duties. I have to make a toast before the dancing begins. Come."

Sammi Jo followed him, to the side of the room. When he got the crowd's attention, he proposed a toast. Sammi Jo felt her throat constrict with emotion. Andy Rafe had a way with words, no doubt about that. And he meant them.

Andrew took her hand. "My official duties are over. Let's dance."

"Don't you have to dance with the bridesmaids?"

"I've discovered that they all came with steady boy-friends or significant others."

"So you didn't need dance lessons after all."

"Oh, I wouldn't say that. One of these days I might get married and have to dance while everyone watches."

"Are you really considering marriage?"

"Why not?"

"After all the marriages you've dissolved in your court, I thought you might be gun-shy."

"Like you?"

"Like me."

"Being gun-shy is something you can overcome. Look at our new couple. This is the second time around for both. Don't they look happy?"

"Yes, but then have you ever seen an unhappy bride and groom? I haven't. The test is whether they'll still be happy ten years down the road."

"Oh, ye of little faith," Andrew said, leading her

onto the dance floor. He placed his arms around her. "They're both older now. More mature. They know what to expect. Don't you think that helps?"

"Definitely." Sammi Jo felt the pressure of Andy Rafe's hand on her back and let herself relax against him. Being older definitely helped. The couple would probably make it. Sammi Jo felt joy rush through her. Joy and something that might be hope and optimism. Briefly she wondered if she'd taken leave of her senses. Why was she linking marriage with hope and optimism? Feeling Andy Rafe's strong arms around her, she refused to analyze her thoughts and feelings. For once, a moment of happiness was enough.

Sammi Jo parked her car in Andy Rafe's driveway. She tried very hard to walk normally, but as soon as she joined her host and her grandfather on the terrace, she knew they had noticed her stiff movements.

"What's wrong, Sugar?" Nate asked.

Suppressing a groan, she bent down to kiss her grandfather's cheek. "Nothing's wrong." Then, gazing at the view, she said, "Oh my. I'm surprised you can ever bear to leave this house, Andy Rafe. If I lived here, I'd probably spend all my time on this terrace."

"The view is even better from over here," he told her.

"Really? It couldn't be." Sammi Jo started toward the far side where Andy Rafe stood next to the barbecue. Halfway there, she realized that he had tricked her.

"Want to tell us again that nothing's wrong?" he asked, his arms crossed over his chest.

"Oh, all right. Greg dropped me. It wasn't his fault," she added hastily, sensing their reaction even before they had a chance to voice it. "We were practicing swing moves and he stumbled over some wires and couldn't catch me."

"What kind of wires?" Andrew asked.

"Electrical. Mr. Manning promised to have an electrician come and fix the wiring, but since you've put him back in jail, he can't very well do that. Though considering that he hasn't repaired anything else, he might not have fixed this either," she admitted exhaustedly.

"Why were the wires sticking out so that Greg tripped on them?" Nate wanted to know.

"Because we needed more room, so we moved the small desk." Seeing her grandfather's uncomprehending frown, she added, "The wires are usually stuck behind the desk, so nobody trips over them." She sighed. "The problem is that the studio just doesn't have enough electrical outlets. When I plug in my boom box, I have to unplug the watercooler or blow a fuse." Sammi Jo caught the look the two men exchanged. "What?" she demanded.

Her grandfather spoke. "It appears to me that the place has a whole lot of things wrong with it. Some of them are even dangerous."

"Not really," she assured him. "I just have to remember not to plug in too many things at the same time." Sammi Jo pressed her hand against her back.

"Are you hurting, Sugar?"

"A little. If the studio had a shower, I'd have stood under the hot water for half an hour and that would have eased the pain considerably," she said, her tone longing.

"I have lots of hot water," Andrew said. "How do

you want it? In a shower? A bathtub? A hot tub?" He saw her eyes open wide in surprise.

"You have a hot tub?"

"And it's all yours."

"Are you serious?"

"The man just offered it to you," Nate said.

"Unless you're so hungry that you'd rather eat—"

"No, no. That hot water sounds heavenly. I'll just get my gym bag from the car."

"Come on upstairs. It's the door at the end of the hall."

Sammi Jo walked as rapidly as she could to fetch her bag. When she came back and located the bathroom, Andy Rafe was waiting with two white towels in his hands.

"I'm so glad you came. I've looked forward to seeing you all day," he said. "I had a great time at the wedding yesterday. You made the event unforgettable for me."

Sammi Jo groaned and took a step back. "Andy Rafe, you have to stop saying such things to me, and you have to stop being so sweet. You're undermining my resolutions." She watched his hazel eyes light up.

"That's encouraging. Which ones am I undermining?"

"The ones about not getting involved, about not being impulsive and ending up kissing you. Those resolutions."

"I have no intention of not sabotaging those wrong-headed notions of yours, and no restraining order can make me cease and desist." His voice had a definite "so there" ring to it.

"Oh yeah? What if I appeal this to a higher court?"

He shook his head. "The appeal would be thrown out as inhumane and cruel."

"You just made this up. Appeal courts don't throw out cases for being inhumane and cruel."

"Oh yeah? Which one of us is the judge here?"

His grin told her that she was right. His grin was also so appealing that it threatened to melt her. Or maybe it was the steam rising from the hot tub. Whatever it was, she was definitely getting hot.

Sobering, he added, his voice husky, "You haven't a chance, Sammi Jo. I intend to pursue you and win you."

"Win me? What am I? A Kewpie doll at the county fair?"

"No, you're the most exasperating, the most adorable, the most desirable woman I've ever met. And I will win you."

"Win me? What exactly does that mean?" Quickly she lifted her hand to stop his reply. "No, don't tell me. Just give me those towels and get out of here before you get yourself into hot water. I'm the only one in here who needs the hot water. Scoot." Sammi Jo placed one hand on his back, playfully pushed him out the door, and closed it behind him.

Thirty minutes later Sammi Jo emerged from the hot tub, dressed in the clothes from her gym bag.

Andrew marveled again how she could look so good wearing jeans, a plain T-shirt, and sandals.

"You feeling better, Sugar?" Nate asked.

"Yes. I feel like a new woman."

"Good. I'll wheel myself in and start the coffee," Nate said.

Sammi Jo joined Andy Rafe who was taking foil-wrapped packets off the grill.

"Thanks for the use of your hot tub. I don't know how I can repay you. Maybe one evening you'll let me cook dinner for you."

"That would be nice, but I'll settle for less. Or more. Depends on how you look at it."

"Somehow I get the feeling that cooking for you would be a whole lot safer than this more-or-less repayment you have in mind."

Pretending to give this some thought, he finally said, "A home-cooked dinner by an excellent chef is tempting, but I think I'll stick with my original choice."

"Which is?" she prompted.

"Nine kisses in a row."

Sammi Jo was too astonished to speak for a second or two. "Nine kisses?"

"In a row."

"Oh, pardon me. Nine kisses in a row." She paused, waiting for him to explain. When he didn't, she said, "This is undoubtedly a dumb question, but why in a row?"

"I'd like to experience the cumulative effect of kissing you."

Again, she stared at him silently.

"I don't think I've ever seen you speechless before," he said.

"Enjoy it, because it doesn't happen very often."

"Oh, I know that, and I am enjoying it. Just as I'm enjoying being with you."

Sammi Jo threw up her hands. "You're doing it again. Saying sweet things. Cut it out."

"Not a chance," he murmured, his voice low and throaty.

Nate appeared in the doorway of the kitchen. "Andrew, the kitchen timer went off."

"Turn the oven off, please. Time to eat."

Only now did Sammi Jo notice that the round glass table was set for three people. "You haven't eaten yet?"

"We decided to wait for you."

"You shouldn't have. If I'd known that, I wouldn't have stayed in the hot tub so long. I'm sorry. You must be starved."

"We had an excellent appetizer a couple of hours ago. What did you call it, Andrew?" Nate asked.

"Bruschetta."

"You know how to make bruschetta?" she asked.

"Of course." Seeing her surprised expression, he grinned. "I'm joking. I know how to *assemble* bruschetta. The chef at Star Lake Resort made the topping. I grilled the bread and then spread it on top. I saved you a piece." Andrew unwrapped one of the smaller foil packets and handed it to her. "The topping is in that glass dish. Help yourself." He pointed to the little table next to the grill.

Sammi Jo heaped the tomato-basil combination on top of the golden grilled bread. Though she wanted to savor the appetizer, she was too hungry to eat it slowly.

"How do you rate the resort chef's bruschetta?" he asked.

"It was excellent. Maybe a half-pinch too much sugar. I like mine more vinegary."

"That figures," Andrew said, sotto voce.

"I heard that." Sammi Jo elbowed him lightly. "You asked my opinion, and by now you know I'm not an eyelash-batting, sweet, submissive, clingy woman."

He chuckled. "Submissive? You? Glory be, Sammi Jo. If you were, you wouldn't find me within a mile of you. I like you just the way you are: a drop or two of vinegar in your disposition along with strength, charm, and determination." Then, so softly that her grandfather couldn't hear, he added, "Though I wouldn't mind you clinging to me a little more now and again."

Though he had said all this lightly, his eyes were filled with an intensity that made Sammi Jo unable to hold his gaze. Her heart beat rapidly. Her hands shook a little when she reached for the bowl of grilled vegetables. She carried them to the table.

Andy Rafe really liked her. She could no longer pretend that he didn't. Odd, though her ex-husband had professed to love her, he had never told her that he liked her. Or she him. If they had liked each other, would they have lasted together?

When they were seated around the table with their plates filled, the men talked of fishing. Sammi Jo continued to ponder what Andy Rafe had said to her.

"Why so serious and quiet, Sugar? More trouble with your landlord?"

"No, Granddad. I was just wondering something." She hesitated briefly before she continued. "You and Grandmother were married a long time. Is it necessary to like the person you marry as well as love her? Or him?"

"Absolutely," Nate said without hesitation. "Young people don't usually believe this, but that first passion cools down after a while, and then if you don't like your mate, what's left? In a good marriage, the partners become friends and companions as well as lovers. At least that's what we believed in my generation.

That's why we always thought that character was so important. Wouldn't you agree, Andrew?"

"Not having been married, I can't speak from experience, but what you said makes sense to me."

"Sammi Jo?" Nate asked, waiting for her opinion.

"I think you're probably right." Then, not wanting to go on with the discussion, she said, "This fish is delicious. My compliments to the chef."

"Thank you. Coming from you, that's high praise. Would you like some more? Though I ought to warn you that we also have dessert."

"And what's for dessert?" she asked eagerly.

"Apple cobbler that's warming in the oven and frozen vanilla yogurt with a pinch of something called cardamom. Both from the resort."

Sammi Jo groaned with anticipated pleasure. Turning to her grandfather she said, "If the yogurt is anywhere near the quality of their ice cream, we're in for a treat." Then remembering her grandfather's diet, she asked, "Is it regular yogurt or low fat?"

"Low fat, but it still tastes great. Trust me—I sampled it."

After the dessert, which turned out to be every bit as delicious as Andrew had promised, they lingered over coffee. The dusk tinged everything with that mauve-blue hue characteristic of twilight in the Blue Ridge Mountains. They watched in reverent silence.

"I may never move again," Sammi Jo said after a while with a satisfied smile.

"As much as I would like you to remain my guest, I'm afraid you will have to move. After you take Nate home, you and I will go to the studio."

"Why?" she asked with a frown.

"Because I want to look at the wiring."

Sammi Jo sat up.

"Sugar," Nate said before she could launch into a spirited reply, "if I had some way to get up those stairs, I'd go to the studio myself."

"You're ganging up on me! You asked Andy Rafe to go with me while I went in the kitchen to get the coffee, didn't you?"

"I volunteered," Andrew said quickly, not wanting Nate to take the blame. Sammi Jo flicked him a disgusted look that clearly indicated they had not exhausted this topic. Knowing her, their exchange later would be heated. That was all right. He didn't even mind arguing with her. He was that far gone. How he could have fallen that hard that fast puzzled him. He was not an impulsive person. Usually he weighed his options and pondered all possible ramifications at length. Except where Sammi Jo was concerned. Heaven help him, for her he had tossed caution to the wind and risked his heart and soul.

Sammi Jo preceded him up the narrow stairway to the studio. She felt tense with anticipation. She wasn't sure what made her more nervous: the possibility of his wanting to collect the promised kisses or his undoubtedly negative reaction to the studio's electrical wiring.

She shut off the alarm, unlocked the door, and flipped the light switch. Nothing happened.

"Drat. Wait here, Andy Rafe. I don't want you to bump into anything." Moving along the wall, she felt her way to the desk where she kept a flashlight. Moments later she had reset the blown fuse and the overhead lights flickered on.

Andy Rafe didn't say anything as he inspected the

fuse box and looked at the light fixtures. When he pulled the desk away from the wall, he groaned.

"These wires look like a tangle of cooked spaghetti."

"That's why I keep them behind the desk so none of my clients will trip over them." She waited for him to speak again, though from his narrow-eyed gaze she knew that whatever he had to say wouldn't be pleasant. "Well?" she finally demanded.

Very calmly he said, "You know as well as I what the answer is. The place needs to be rewired." She looked so disheartened that he was tempted to hug her. He stopped himself. Instead he said, "Since you're not the owner, you don't have to pay for the rewiring. Get your attorney to write a letter threatening litigation if Manning doesn't make the promised repairs and bring the premises up to safety standards."

"Will that work?"

"It should. But it will take time." Andrew didn't add that he had no intention of waiting for a potential lawsuit to make its way through the legal system while she continued to teach in a veritable tinderbox. But she didn't need to know that yet. She wouldn't like his interference, not even when she found out that he had Nate's full support. She had guessed right: they were ganging up on her, but it was for her own good. They both cared about her and couldn't idly stand by while she was in danger.

"If you've seen all you want to see, we should go. Tomorrow is a work day." Sammi Jo moved toward the door.

They had driven to the studio in her car. Something about the car now seemed odd to Sammi Jo, but before she realized what it was, she heard Andy Rafe groan.

"Flat tires," he muttered.

"Two flat tires? Both the front and the rear are flat? Just great. I have only one spare! Why am I always so lucky?"

Andrew walked to the passenger side of her car. He shook his head.

"What?" Sammi Jo asked.

"You have four flat tires."

Sammi Jo ran around the car to stand next to him. "How can all of my tires be flat at the same time? That's not possible!"

"Ordinarily it isn't."

"Are you saying somebody deliberately let the air out of my tires?"

"What other explanation is there? The odds of all four tires going flat at the same time must be—"

"That lamebrained Junior and his no-neck cousin!" Sammi Jo kicked the nearest flat tire.

"What makes you think it was them?" Andrew asked.

"Because Junior put that note. . . ." She swallowed the rest of the sentence, but judging from Andrew's expression, he wasn't about to ignore her slip of the tongue.

"What note?"

She shrugged. "It was nothing."

Andrew placed his hands on her shoulders, forcing her to face him. "What note? And don't tell me it was nothing."

"He's been after me to move out of the studio."

"You told me that. What did the note say?"

"Can't we just not have this conversation? I need to call the garage—"

"In a minute. First, let's talk about this."

"There isn't much to talk about."

"Try again. You're upset about something Junior wrote. What was it?"

"You're going to be stubborn about this, aren't you?"

"As stubborn as a Missouri mule. You may as well just tell me."

Sammi Jo sighed. In a resigned tone she said, "It's no big deal. Junior wrote a note and put it under the windshield wiper. At least I'm ninety-nine percent sure it was him."

"Did you take the note to the police?"

"No. I told you I have no proof that it was him."

Forcing himself to remain calm, Andrew asked, "Do you still have the note?"

"Yes. It's in the glove compartment." Sammi Jo unlocked the car and removed the note. She unfolded it and held it out to him.

"Put it on the hood, please. I don't want to contaminate the evidence any more than it already has been."

Sammi Jo's patience snapped. "Oh, for heaven's sake! I'm sure Junior wasn't dumb enough to leave fingerprints on it."

"You'd be surprised how dumb a lot of criminals are."

Sammi Jo watched him read the note. When he looked up at her, his expression seemed to be a mixture of shock and anger.

"You didn't take this seriously?" he asked, his voice filled with disbelief.

She shrugged. "Junior strikes me as being full of himself. Sort of a minor bully. Letting the air out of my tires is just about his speed."

"I'm sure he started out as a bully, but Junior has

graduated to more serious crimes. From misdemeanors to felonies. He's nobody to toy with, Sammi Jo." Though it was hard to tell in the poorly lit parking lot, he thought her face had turned pale.

"Maybe I underestimated him, but I could have sworn he looked at me as if I were nothing more than a nuisance."

"Maybe so," Andrew said, not wanting to alarm her further, "but stay out of his way and always leave with your students in the evening. Don't stay here alone. Promise. If you don't, I'll have to come here every evening to see you safely on your way."

"You wouldn't!" Seeing the determined angle of his jaw, she added, "Would you?"

"Try me."

"All right. I promise to leave with my students. I've been doing that anyway."

"Good. Let's call the tow truck," he added, his voice gentle. "It shouldn't take them long to get here."

After Sammi Jo made the call using her cell phone, she said thoughtfully, "I still don't understand why Junior wants the studio. He has the downstairs to store his car parts."

"Is that what he uses the place for? How do you know that? Have you been spying on him after I told you—"

"No, I didn't spy on him. I saw him and his cousin carry fenders inside one evening. I'd come back down to get something from my car."

"Did they see you?"

"No. I thought they acted sort of sneaky as if they didn't want anyone to see them carry in those Corvette parts, so I waited until they'd entered the building before I raced back upstairs."

"Sammi Jo, how do you know those were Corvette parts? I wouldn't have pegged you as a woman who'd recognize car fenders."

"Corvette fenders are the only ones I recognize because my ex-husband owned a 'Vette. I declare that car was more precious to him than anything else on this entire planet. We'd sometimes park blocks from a restaurant even though there were parking spots a lot nearer simply because those didn't look safe to him. I'm not talking about a possible scratch or little dent, though that would have been a catastrophe too. He was terrified that someone would steal the car. I guess he did have some justification for his paranoia since Corvettes are stolen with great frequency. . . ." Sammi Jo's voice trailed off as the realization hit her.

She met Andy Rafe's gaze and saw the same realization in his eyes.

"That would explain why Junior doesn't want anyone in the studio," he said. "You might inadvertently see just what you did see the other night. That he's running a chop shop."

"I wondered at the time why he didn't take them to his place, but if they're stolen—"

"Sammi Jo, promise you won't reveal any of your suspicions to Junior." When she opened her mouth to protest, he laid his hand lightly over it. "Promise to act as if you don't suspect a thing. Nod yes, Sammi Jo."

She did.

"I'll handle it. You go on as if nothing happened." He put his arms around her and drew her deeper into the shadows. He backed her against one of the dark lampposts.

"What are you up to?" she asked.

"I thought while we wait, we might work on those nine kisses you promised me. Any objections?"

"I don't suppose it would do any good if I wanted to take this under advisement?" she asked.

"No. That's the prerogative of the judge. You could ask for a postponement, but do you really want to wait?"

"Would you grant me a postponement?"

"Nope."

She sighed exaggeratedly. "Well, in that case we might as well get this over with."

"Such enthusiasm is really encouraging to a man."

She smiled at his pseudo-hurt tone. "I've never thought of you as a man who discouraged easily."

"I don't. Not when I really want something, and I want you."

"Are you sure about that? Once you have me, you might be disappointed."

"No way." He traced the shape of her mouth with this thumb. He felt her inhale and hold her breath.

"Or you might not know what to do with me," she added. "I've been told that I'm not easy to get along with."

"I bet Nate didn't tell you that, and since you get along just fine with your grandfather, and I with him, it follows that you and I should get along as well." Andrew's fingers caressed her throat. He felt her pulse jump and his own skyrocketed.

"Is this one of those if-A-then-B-and-therefore-C arguments? I was never very good at logical deduction," she said, her voice shaky.

"Syllogisms." Andrew couldn't take his eyes off her lush lips until they parted slightly, causing heat to rush through his body. "I'm good at deductive reasoning.

Or I usually am, but being this close to you, my thoughts grow fuzzy." He drew her closer, even though that threatened a shutdown of all logical thought processes.

Sammi Jo seemed to have lost control over her arms as they spontaneously encircled his shoulders. Her fingers inched up to stroke his hair which felt soft and silky. A deeply pleasurable sensation surged through her fingertips. She thought she could stroke Andy Rafe's hair for hours, until he pressed her body against his. He had held her while they had danced, and he had kissed her before, but his touch, his kiss, were entirely different now. This was Andy Rafe as she had never known him: all primitive male, demanding, hungry, possessive.

He tasted of coffee and cardamom and something that was just him, undefinable and unforgettable. With every breath she took his scent flowed through her, exhilarating and arousing, quickening her heart and pulse but numbing her mind with exquisite pleasure until nothing existed but a vortex of pure emotion and sensation.

As if muffled by the sound of breaking waves, she heard voices. Andy Rafe broke the kiss but held her for a moment longer. She became aware that his breathing was as labored as hers.

"We'll never last through nine kisses in a row," she murmured.

"I think we will, but we'll definitely have to work on our pacing." He took a deep, steadying breath before he turned toward the tow truck.

Chapter Eight

Although Sammi Jo hired a professional maid service to do the heavy cleaning in the studio, she performed the between-visit dusting and mopping. Usually she did these chores in the early morning, but on Monday she overslept. That was Andy Rafe's fault. His kiss had agitated and worried her so that she hadn't been able to fall asleep until the early hours of the morning.

On Tuesday morning she arrived at the studio extra early to catch up on the cleaning. When she saw the pickup in the parking lot, she frowned. It wasn't Junior's pickup, which had extra big tires and sat high off the ground. This one was plastered with bumper stickers with messages that made her cringe. Whose was it, and why was it parked here?

She approached the pickup just as two men came around front from behind the building. Something about them caused Sammi Jo to stick her hand into her large shoulder bag and locate her cell phone, ready to dial 911 should the men make a threatening move toward her. They seemed to be as surprised to see her as she was to find them there.

"Good morning. Can I help you gentlemen?" They stared at her unblinkingly. Sammi Jo became acutely aware of the empty parking lot. It would be an hour yet before the little grocery store across the street opened. Masking her unease, she asked, "Who are you, and what are you doing here?"

"We could ask you the same thing," the cadaverously thin man said, his voice weak. He took two steps toward her.

The downward slant of his mouth gave his bony face a mean look. He reminded her of a hungry junkyard dog. Sammi Jo envisioned the buttons on her cell phone. Her fingers pressed 911—or what she hoped was the emergency number.

"My studio is in this building which is located on the corner of Main and Laurel. Is that the site you were looking for?" She hoped the operator had caught the address.

The second men, shorter and stockier, said, "We got business here, honey. Why don't you just mosey along like a good little girl."

Sammi Jo bristled at being called a good little girl but held her temper. Judging by the speaker's crooked nose and missing upper front teeth, he appeared to be a man who'd seen his share of fistfights. As calmly as she could, she said, "I work here. Do you work for Junior Manning?"

Both men laughed as if her question were the funniest thing they'd ever heard.

"That's a good 'un. Us working for Junior. You working for that shiftless jackrabbiter?"

"No. I just rent the upstairs studio from him. I'm

Sammi Jo Crawford. Who are you?" Toothless answered her.

"That don't matter. I didn't think you was working for Junior. Or that you was his woman. Him bein' ugly enough to bust a mirror, he'd never get his hands on somebody like you, honey. Me and my brother here, we know how to show a woman a good time."

Sammi Jo didn't like the way the conversation was going. Fortunately a police siren cut through the morning stillness.

The men exchanged a look, jumped into the truck, and took off.

She waited until the squad car arrived to tell the officer what had happened.

"Can you describe the men, Miss Crawford?"

She did. Then she added, "They obviously didn't like Junior. They called him a jackrabbiter. What's that?"

"Somebody who makes inferior moonshine."

"I didn't know moonshine could be ranked by quality," she murmured. Andy Rafe had been right in suspecting the Mannings of making illegal liquor. "Do you know who the men are?"

The officer nodded. "Sounds like the Whittaker brothers."

"The ones feuding with the Mannings?"

"Yes. You said they came from the back of the building?"

Sammi Jo nodded. She waited while the officer went to investigate.

When he returned a few minutes later, he said, "I didn't find anything. Your early arrival probably kept them from doing whatever they'd planned to do."

"Like what?"

"Last time they feuded, they set each other's places on fire."

Sammi Jo gasped. When her heartbeat slowed she asked, "Was anyone hurt in the fires?"

"Fortunately not. They set the fires in the middle of the night when no one was there. To be on the safe side we'll swing by here in the morning just as we do in the evening, even though the judge hasn't asked us to do so. But you be careful, Miss Crawford. Dialing 911 was a smart move."

The officer was gone before Sammi Jo got her wits together enough to ask which judge had asked them to patrol the parking lot. As if she didn't know! Part of her was pleased by Andy Rafe's concern, but part of her resented it. She didn't need looking after. Well, maybe she could use some help, what with the feud apparently starting again and conceivably involving arson. However, she preferred being asked whether she wanted protection rather than having it forced on her. She'd have to talk to Andy Rafe about this, but not yet. She wasn't quite ready to face him, not after the last two days, which had thrown her poise and peace of mind into total turmoil.

Ready or not, two days later Andy Rafe stopped by the studio during his lunch recess. He'd had two sack lunches delivered to his office from the resort's kitchen.

"You're early. The invitation to dinner with Grand-dad and me wasn't until tonight," she said, her tone overly light, her smile bright. He didn't smile back. His hazel eyes, which usually looked at her with a warm expression, regarded her coolly. Sammi Jo discovered that she preferred the warm expression.

"Your reaction is becoming predictable. Every time we get close, you then avoid me like the plague," Andrew told her. "I wouldn't have thought that predictability was one of your traits."

"I don't think it is. Except with you," she admitted.

"Do I scare you?" Andrew asked with a worried frown.

"No. Not exactly."

"At least that's something," he said, his tone dry. Andrew waited for her to explain. She looked skittish, ready to bolt. He couldn't let her. "Sammi Jo, talk to me. If I don't scare you, then why do you avoid me?"

"You confuse me. You upset the balance of my life."

He stared at her. Finally he said, "You're going to have to explain that to me."

"I'll try." She took a deep breath. "When I came back to Pine Springs, I knew exactly what I wanted and what I had to do to get it. I wanted to take care of my grandfather, and I wanted to create an independent, self-supporting life for myself that centered around dancing."

"And that life didn't include me."

"It didn't include *any* man."

"What's so awful about having a man in your life? I don't understand what's so terrifying about being in a relationship."

"That's because you haven't been down that road before."

"What makes you think that we'd be traveling down that exact same road? I'm not like your ex-husband, and you're not the same woman you were when you married him. You can't deny that."

"I don't. Still, that road is full of potential pain and failure. I'm not sure I'm ready for that again."

"Sammi Jo, the operative word here is *potential*. One precedent isn't enough to base a judgment on. Besides, isn't a loving relationship worth the risk?"

She shrugged. "I've failed in one relationship already."

"That doesn't mean you're doomed to fail again." Andrew took a deep breath. "I'd never hurt you. At least not deliberately," he added quickly when he saw her doubtful expression. "I would not hold you back, or control you, or interfere with your dancing or anything else you wanted to do, as long as you were safe. I swear it. Take a chance on me. On us."

She sighed deeply and shrugged. The gesture immediately revealed how hard it was for her to believe and trust him. Just then Andrew wanted nothing more than to get his hands on her ex-husband, that miserable excuse for a man. Putting these vengeful thoughts aside, he debated how he could convince her.

"Sammi Jo, you're not a coward. I know that. Nate told me that you refused alimony and walked away from your marriage with nothing but your clothes. And you wouldn't accept financial help from him or your parents. You started your studio on a shoestring. That takes guts. You're taking a risk there, so why not take a risk with us?"

"Because if I fail with the studio, it'll hurt, but it won't rip my insides apart."

"Neither will I."

She shook her head. "Brave, foolish words. The way we react to each other—"

"And how's that?" he asked.

"Like a lit match flung into an open powder keg."

"A good description." Andrew nodded thoughtfully. "I think I understand. What you're really afraid of is this powerful force between us."

"No. Well, maybe. If you had any sense, it would scare you too."

Andrew grinned at her. "I think that explosive pull, the way we feel when we touch and kiss, is wonderful."

"Being a man, you would think that."

"If you're honest, Sammi Jo, you'll admit that the physical chemistry isn't the only thing that draws us to each other. We have a good time together. We're compatible. Our traits are complementary. We hold the same values. Can you dispute that?"

She shook her head but didn't say anything. She didn't even look at him. He waited. When she didn't speak he asked, "Is that what's really troubling you? You could accept the physical, maybe, but not the other? The fact that we like each other? Am I—"

"Don't even say anything as ridiculous as not being good enough. I won't hear it!" She looked at him with stormy eyes and a fierce expression.

"Okay, I won't say it, but explain to me what's troubling you. I'm obviously particularly dense today."

"This physical thing that explodes each time we touch each other is worrisome. Heaven only knows where it could lead us," she said.

To paradise, Andrew thought, but was prudent enough not to say it out loud.

"If kisses were the only thing, I could ignore them," she said. "Well, probably. But they aren't. As you said, we really have a great time together. And if that were the only thing, we could be friends, and there'd be no problem. But when we add the compatibility to the attraction, we've got trouble."

"You lost me. What you consider trouble, I consider a blessing," Andrew said.

"That's because you've never been in a marriage that went wrong. This attraction can be more of a curse than a blessing. People do terrible things to people in the name of love. Believe me, I know."

Andrew took her hand and held it, even though she tried to pull it away. "You're wrong. Not about the terrible things people do to each other, I see that in my court all the time. But you're wrong about that having been done with love. Real love is the most selfless quality in the universe. Real love is unconditional." Andrew raised her hand and kissed it.

She looked at him with wide, astonished eyes. Eyes in which he could lose himself forever. With every ounce of self-discipline at his command, he said, "I brought lunch. Let's eat."

He set the two sacks on the desk. "Please join me. The chef made up a special lunch. Very healthy, he told me. Something a dancer would like." Andrew took two jars from the sack. "One is filled with hummus and the other with . . . something ghanoush. Not that I have any idea what either of those is."

She swooped down on the jar, took it, and looked at it with sheer delight. "I haven't had baba ghanoush since I left Atlanta! I love it."

"What is it?

"It's an eggplant dish."

Andrew grinned at her. "You're the only person I know who gets that enthusiastic about eggplant."

"You don't like eggplant?"

He shrugged. "I'm not sure whether I've ever eaten

any. All I know is that it's kind of a homely looking vegetable."

"It is not! It has a shiny, deep purple skin that's most unusual. I'll have you know that designers name fashion colors after it. They usually call it 'aubergine.' What else is in those bags?"

"Iced tea, raw vegetables and. . . ." He frowned at the plastic bag, then held it up for her to see.

"Pitas cut into triangles. Lovely," she said.

"And raisin oatmeal cookies for dessert. Those, at least, I recognize," he said.

Sammi Jo set out the paper plates, plastic forks, and spoons and napkins. Andrew pulled up a chair.

"This bubba stuff isn't half bad," he said after tasting it.

Sammi Jo laughed. "Not bubba. It's spelled b-a-b-a. The dish is from the Middle East. I'm glad you like it."

"See, I'm even beginning to like the strange foods you eat," he told her. "Doesn't that speak volumes in our favor? If I argued our case before a jury, they'd unanimously find in our favor."

"But if I argued against us—"

"You'd lose the case," he said with conviction.

"What monumental confidence! I thought lawyers couldn't guess how a jury might vote."

"True, but I wouldn't be guessing. I'm absolutely sure of our case and, therefore, of the jury's verdict."

"Must be nice to be so certain," she said with a sigh.

"I realize that you have trouble trusting and believing because of the past, but think of it as having happened long ago and far away. In another lifetime. You and I are new, and everything is possible." Andrew leaned toward her. He brushed a crumb from the corner of her mouth and leaned even closer.

"What are you doing?" she asked, trying to lean back, but his hand moved lightning quick to her neck and gently stopped her.

"We have eight kisses to go. Have you forgotten?"

"No, but this is the middle of the day!"

"There's no law against kissing in the middle of the day. I looked that up before I came." That rated him a smile.

"Do the taxpayers know for what frivolous research their money is used?" she asked.

"Sure. You have no idea what obscure and arcane laws we still have on the books that I have to look up and rule on."

"How would you rule on kissing in the middle of the day?"

He grinned. "How do you think? I'd give tax credits for it. Just think how much less violence there'd be if people spent their time kissing instead of fighting."

His eyes were smiling at her in a way that made her feel warm and tingly. She had to remind him, as much as herself, of where they were. "Andy Rafe, I've got a dance class in a little while, and doesn't court resume soon too? I don't know how good an idea it is to—"

"It's an excellent idea. What you have to remember is that there are as many different kinds of kisses as there are occasions for them. For example, there's sweet and gentle just right for the middle of the day," he whispered, and lowered his head to demonstrate.

Though the kiss was as sweet and gentle as he'd promised, it packed enough heat to leave them both breathless when they broke apart.

Before either could say anything, the phone rang.

They both glanced at her phone before Andy Rafe said, "My cell phone, I believe."

While he answered it, Sammi Jo cleared the desk. The lunch had been delicious and she was deeply touched that Andy Rafe had gone to so much trouble. She didn't pay any attention to his conversation until she sensed a change in tone. When she met his steely gaze, she knew she was in trouble. *Now what,* she wondered.

"Why is it that I always have to learn of the trouble you get yourself in from others?" he asked, putting the phone into his jacket pocket.

"What trouble?" she demanded, feeling defensive.

"The Whittakers. Remember their early morning visit?"

"There wasn't much to tell, and what there was, I told the police. Wasn't that the right thing to do?"

"Yes, but why didn't you tell me?"

"I was going to tonight. I didn't expect you to show up at noon with lunch, which was delicious, and then get into kissing, and. . . ." She shrugged. Then she frowned. "Who told you? That's the trouble with small towns. Everybody knows about everybody's business. Do you have spies all over town? Am I under surveillance? Isn't that an invasion of my privacy?"

"Slow down, please. It's not you who's under surveillance. I just don't want you caught in the middle of a feud."

"Why would I be? Neither side is interested in me."

"Bystanders get hurt in feuds too."

"The police officer told me that no one was hurt in the fires, so even if they decide to torch the building in the middle of the night, I won't be here."

Andrew reached for her hand. Pressing it for emphasis, he said, "It's true that no one was hurt in the fires, but the man starting the bomb-rigged car wasn't so lucky, and neither was the woman who was hit by a stray bullet. She spent a long time in physical therapy."

"And the man?"

"He died."

"Oh. I'll be careful. I'll be all right," Sammi Jo said, her voice firm.

She didn't know just how safe he planned for her to be. Knowing Sammi Jo, she wasn't going to like what he'd planned one bit. Heck, that was an enormous understatement. She was going to be absolutely furious with him. But she would be safe, and that was most important. Hopefully she'd get over her anger quickly.

Thinking it prudent to change the subject, he asked, "So? What are you cooking for us tonight?"

"A pasta dish. With chicken, not tofu. You'll like it."

"I'm sure I will. I'll bring frozen yogurt. Low fat," he added quickly. Andrew paused, choosing his words carefully. "Sammi Jo, remember that all issues have two sides. In my job I see that all the time."

"I realize that. Why do you think it necessary to tell me that?"

"Well, if, for example, you got upset with me. Please remember that there are two sides to the argument."

"Andy Rafe, just what are you planning to do to make me upset with you?"

"I was just speaking hypothetically," he said quickly.

"Oh. You're still holding the prom against me. I am sorry about that Andy Rafe. If I could undo—"

"You can't, but I don't hold it against you anymore." He'd already forgiven her for that long-ago incident. What he was worried about now was the incident which was scheduled to happen in the next few days. Just to refresh her memory of how good they were together, he had to kiss her once more before he left.

Her doorbell rang. He stopped her with his hand on her arm.

"My students—"

"They can wait a moment." Molding her body against his, he kissed her the way a man kissed a woman for whom he would risk his heart and soul. She responded the way he'd hoped she would, plunging him into a pleasure so acute it bordered on torment.

The doorbell rang insistently.

"I hate to let you go, but you'd better open the door," he whispered hoarsely.

Sammi Jo turned the tape off before the song had even ended. It wasn't right for her Saturday class at the community center. She was finally getting the teenagers to participate in ballroom dancing with a small degree of enthusiasm and didn't want to jeopardize the progress she had made by selecting the wrong music.

They were a tough group. Maybe not really even all that tough, but uncertain and scared, which they covered up by copping an attitude.

After watching a couple of dance competition videos, the teens had picked the dances they wanted to learn. That they had voted for the rumba didn't surprise her, for the dance was romantic, rhythmic, and, thanks to all that hip action, sexy. She had felt compelled though to warn them that the quick step, which they had chosen because it looked like fun, called for lots of stamina and energy. They had swaggeringly assured her that they had tons of each. At their age she had probably felt just as confident and invincible.

The doorbell interrupted her music search. Sammi Jo glanced at her watch. It was too early for her next class. Was it Andy Rafe? He had taken to appearing unexpectedly and frequently of late, throwing her into a tizzy. Somehow they always ended up in each other's arms.

It wasn't as if Andy Rafe hadn't warned her, but even knowing that he was so serious about "winning" her, as he put it, she hadn't been able to resist him. Could she possibly be falling in love with the man? That thought made her pause on the stairs. No, surely not. Hadn't she sworn never to fall in love again?

The answer was simple. She hadn't really dated anyone in over two years. She was a little lonely and naturally that made her vulnerable to the first man who managed to sneak past her primary line of defense. And if that man had the determination and the appeal of Andy Rafe, she couldn't help but be attracted to him. That, of course, was a long way from falling in love with him. She was still safe if she remained vigilant and curbed her natural impulsiveness.

The doorbell rang again. Sammi Jo ran down the rest of the stairs, looked through the peephole, and felt a crushing letdown. The man on the other side of the door wasn't Andy Rafe. She disarmed the alarm and opened the door.

Seeing the visitor's badge, she asked, "Is there a fire?"

"No. I'm here to inspect the premises as required by law. May I come up?"

"Of course." Sammi Jo motioned for him to go on up. She hadn't known that the fire marshal's office inspected business establishments, though that made sense.

She followed him. When she reached the loft, she found the inspector standing in the middle of the room. He turned slowly, looking around. Sammi Jo tried to see the loft through his eyes. She thought the place looked good: the wooden floor was shiny, the mirrors were unsmudged, the plants were colorful. Her desk was uncluttered. Everything was clean. She smiled, pleased, until she saw his face. Why did he have that . . . amazed look on his face? And what was he writing on the form on his clipboard? A rush of anxiety filled her.

The inspector walked to the window and looked down. Slowly he paced the perimeter of the room, frequently making notations on his form. Sammi Jo was decidedly uneasy now.

"Is something wrong?" she finally asked.

"Wrong? Miss Crawford, that word doesn't begin to describe what I'm seeing here."

Bewildered, she glanced around the room again. It still looked just fine to her. "I'm sorry, but I don't understand. What's wrong with this studio?"

"For openers, a room this size needs two exits. That's the law. If there were a fire in here, only half the people would have a chance of getting out. If that many."

Sammi Jo felt faint. "Two exits? I didn't know that."

"There's no fire escape, and I don't see any fire extinguishers." He made more notes.

This was not good. "My landlord didn't tell me any of these things. He said the building was licensed for commercial use."

"Maybe the ground floor is, but there's no way the upstairs would have passed inspection. You can be sure I'll check on the downstairs premises as soon as I can."

The inspector checked the fuse box. He turned on some lamps. Sammi Jo prayed he wouldn't see the unplugged water-cooler and . . . too late. He plugged the watercooler in and promptly the lights went out. He didn't say anything, but his expression—the tight lips, the frowning eyes—made words unnecessary. She was in trouble. When he walked toward her desk and pulled it away from the wall, Sammi Jo held her breath.

"The wiring in this place is a firefighter's nightmare." He shook his head. "I'm afraid I'm going to have to close you down until the necessary modifications and repairs have been made."

"What? You can't be serious! You can't do that!"

"I have to. If there had been just one violation or only a couple of minor ones, I could have allowed you to continue here while the repairs were being made. But the place violates all safety codes."

"I've been here for months and nothing has happened," she pointed out.

"You were very lucky. Miss Crawford, have you ever pulled a body from a fire? Or seen one that's been burned to a crisp?"

Sammi Jo swallowed hard and shook her head.

"Believe me, you don't want to see one. And I don't want to pull what's left of you out of the smoking ruins of this firetrap."

"How soon are you closing me down?"

"Right now."

"No! I'm expecting twenty women for aerobics in less than half an hour. I can't possibly notify all of them before they leave home."

"I'm sorry, and I sympathize, but I have no choice."

Shocked, Sammi Jo sat down heavily in her chair. She couldn't afford to cancel the class, and she knew of no other place she could use.

"I'll put the notice on the downstairs door."

Sammi Jo roused herself. Suddenly a number of questions popped into her mind. "As I said, I've been holding classes up here for several months. What made you suddenly decide to inspect the studio? Did Junior Manning put you up to this? He's been trying to get me to leave."

The inspector looked truly offended. "Ma'am, I wouldn't spit on Junior Manning if he were on fire, if you'll forgive the crude expression."

"Then who told you about the wiring? Someone had to have told you. You went straight to that desk. You knew about the wires behind it before you saw them."

"I've got to go," the inspector said and fumbled while tearing off the duplicate copy of his report.

"Jumping jive! It has to be him. It was Judge Garroway, wasn't it?" she demanded.

The inspector placed the report on her desk. He couldn't meet her gaze. "I'm only doing my job," he said and all but sprinted to the door.

"Andy Rafe, how could you?" she murmured brokenheartedly while tears ran down her cheeks. He had wooed her, pursued her, sweet-talked her, kissed her, and all the time he had been plotting to close her studio. She couldn't wait to get to the bottom of this. That high and mighty judge would rue the day he'd decided to take control of her life.

Sammi Jo snatched her bag and keys and ran to her car.

When she arrived at the courthouse, she found out that Andy Rafe had just left for home. His secretary told her he left early because a case had been continued, whatever that meant. Sammi Jo was too upset to ask for details. She took off for his place.

All the way there she held her anger under tight control, not wanting to cause an accident. She found him outside, getting ready to mow his lawn. He wore only cutoffs and sneakers. He looked good. Very good. For some reason that only fueled her anger.

Out of habit, Sammi Jo grabbed her bag as she got out of the car, even though she didn't bother to shut off the engine or close the door. She stormed toward Andy Rafe who waited for her, a welcoming, expectant smile on his face. When she halted a couple of steps from him, his smile faded.

"You! You. . . ." She had to stop to take a breath. "There aren't enough ugly words in the English language to describe what I think of you. You sicced the fire inspector on me, didn't you? Don't even try to deny it."

"All right, I won't deny it, but—"

"How could you do this to me? I trusted you." In impotent anger Sammi Jo threw her bag at him. He caught it.

"I didn't want you to burn up in that fire hazard of a studio."

"If I choose to burn up, that's my business."

"Sammi Jo, that doesn't make any sense."

"Yes, it does. I'm a grown woman. I'm allowed to make my own choices and my own mistakes—"

"Not when they endanger you. How do you think the people who care about you would feel if something happened to you? Nate and I—"

"Leave my grandfather out of this."

"Okay," he said, lifting his hand in a conciliatory manner. "But if you think I'll stand by and watch you run risks that threaten your life, you can think again. I care about you—"

"Ha! You're just like my ex-husband and my father. No, you're worse. They at least never pretended to be something they weren't. I can't believe I was that fooled by you." Despite heroic efforts to hold back the tears, she felt them course down her cheeks. That upset her even more.

"Aw, Sammi Jo, don't cry. It breaks my heart. I—"

"Andrew, you don't have a heart."

"I like it better when you call me Andy Rafe."

When he took a step toward her, she cried, "Stay away from me. Don't you dare touch me."

"You don't mean that. You're overreacting."

"What if I am? Don't I have a right to react and overreact after what you've done? You said you would never control me, you'd never interfere—"

"As long as you were safe. I'm sure you remember that I added that caveat."

"Caveat? Don't you use your legal jargon on me." Sammi Jo's voice failed her. Tears streamed down her face. It took all her strength not to sob out loud. She ran toward her car.

"Sammi Jo, wait!"

She kept on running.

Andrew started after her, but stopped when he realized that whatever he did or said would only upset her more. He didn't want her to end up in a ditch again.

"We'll talk about this when you've calmed down."

Helplessly he watched her drive away. He felt shaken clear down to his toes. He had known she would be angry, but he hadn't anticipated that she would be this devastated. Each of her words had bitten into him like the flick of a whip. Heck, he'd gladly take a whipping if it would spare Sammi Jo such unhappiness.

Fleetingly Andrew wondered if he'd done the right thing. Then he nodded to himself. He had. He couldn't leave the woman he loved in a place that might harm her. Even kill her. But maybe there had been a better way of doing this. Except neither he nor Nate had found it.

Andrew went inside to call her grandfather.

Chapter Nine

Nate waited for his granddaughter in the front hall.

"Sammi Jo, we have to talk," he said when she walked in. Her face was pale. It was obvious she had been crying.

"Not now, Granddad," she said softly.

"Andrew called me. I know what happened."

"You know his side. I'd hardly call that knowing what happened. I still can't believe he did this to me. I lost the studio because of him. I worked so hard to get my business started." Sammi Jo's voice faltered. New tears flowed from her eyes. She ran upstairs.

"Have yourself a good cry. Then we'll talk," Nate called after her.

Nate wheeled himself into the kitchen. Grunting, he pulled himself into a standing position at the sink to fill the teakettle. He set out the porcelain cups she liked, sliced a lemon, and placed several almond honey cookies on a plate. He waited five more minutes before he called to her.

"There's nothing to talk about," she called back in reply.

"Yes, there is. You've suffered a setback, but you haven't lost the battle, so get yourself down here, Samantha Josephine."

Her grandfather rarely called her by her full name, but when he did, he was dead serious. She splashed her face with cold water before she joined him in the kitchen.

"I made us some tea," Nate said and poured her a cup.

"Thank you." Sammi Jo sipped the hot, golden liquid gratefully.

"Sugar, you look like a gardenia the day after the ball."

"Gee, thanks. You know how to make a girl feel special," Sammi Jo said and almost smiled.

"That's better."

"I haven't cried this much in a long time. I feel like a whole bouquet of used gardenias—wilted, bruised and brown around the edges."

"I know losing the studio is hard—"

"Hard? Granddad, it's my business, my life. It's how I earn my living."

"And you blame Andrew for causing you to lose it."

"Shouldn't I? He blew the whistle on me."

"You feel betrayed."

"Of course, I do. He pretended. . . ." She broke off and bit her lower lip, which was quivering.

"To care about you?" he prompted. When she nodded, Nate said, "Sugar, he does. Maybe he hasn't told you, but he surely does."

"Yeah, right. He has an odd way of showing it."

"And if you didn't care about him, what he did

wouldn't upset you nearly as much," Nate pointed out gently.

"Care about him? Right now I'd like to deck him."

"Seems to me you already tried that. He told me you threw your bag at him."

"For all the satisfaction it gave me," she said angrily. "You know what hurts most of all? The fact that he pretended to be a liberated male, a man who would never do anything as heavy-handed as controlling or manipulating a woman. And then that's exactly what he did."

"Sugar, I have a confession to make. Andrew isn't the only one who's guilty."

"What are you saying?"

"If I had found a way to get myself up to the studio to see firsthand the kind of electrical wiring you mentioned, I would have called the fire marshal myself."

"Granddad—"

"Let me finish, please. Andrew kept urging you to look for a different place, didn't he?"

"Well, yes," she admitted reluctantly.

"But you wouldn't, and after we found out that not only might you be caught in the middle of a feud, but might be trapped in a fire, we knew we had to get you out any way we could. I'm sorry we couldn't think of a less hurtful way of doing it."

"I can't believe you were in on this!" Sammi Jo tried to get up, but her grandfather reached out and stopped her.

"I'm not proud of what I did, but you know what? Under the same circumstances I'd have to do it again." Nate paused. Then he lifted his hand to forestall Sammi Jo's outburst.

"Listen to me. After I became a father, I learned

that the most dreadful thing I could imagine was losing my child. And the prospect of losing my granddaughter is even more hideous. It defies the natural order. I know I wouldn't want to go on living if you didn't. I also know this doesn't excuse my interfering, but I hope it'll explain it."

Sammi Jo sat quietly for several seconds. Then she said, "Maybe it does."

"Don't you think you were overly hard on Andrew? That you overreacted?"

Sammi Jo opened her mouth to refute this claim, but after a moment's thought she changed her mind. "Maybe I did overreact," she admitted.

"Maybe?"

"Oh, all right. I did." She rubbed her forehead. "I can't think. I have such a headache. I'm going to take some aspirin and call my clients to cancel today's sessions. Then I'll hit the pavement to look for another place." Wearily she placed her palms on the table and pushed herself out of the chair.

"You're not giving up. Good for you."

Sammi Jo straightened her shoulders. "You didn't think I would, did you?"

"No, not really. We may have a lead on a place for you."

"We? Who's we?"

"Andrew and I."

"I'm not ready to talk to that man. I'm still upset with him."

"There's an old saying I'd like to remind you of."

"I know I shouldn't ask, but what old saying?"

"Never let the sun set on your anger."

"That's a lot easier said than done." Sammi Jo

squeezed her grandfather's arm. "I better go. I have a lot to do."

She called her answering service. After Lucinda stopped making appropriately sympathetic remarks, she promised to call all clients to cancel classes for the rest of the week.

Thank heaven that some of her classes met at other locations. These lessons would earn her enough income to cover her car and health insurance. She had a little money in the bank, enough to pay for gas and her share of groceries for a couple of months or so, but after that. . . . Sammi Jo shook her head. She couldn't afford to dwell on her financial problems. Better to try to solve them. Besides, feeling sorry for herself wasn't in her nature.

She flipped through the classified section of the newspaper and copied down two addresses that sounded vaguely promising.

It took her an hour to find the first one and only a few minutes to dismiss it as completely unsuitable. The second one wasn't any better.

Discouraged, she returned home where she found her grandfather in bed. It was so unlike him to be lying down in the middle of the day that Sammi Jo rushed to his side.

"What's wrong, Granddad? Shall I call the doctor? An ambulance?"

"Hold on, Sugar. I just felt a little under the weather, so I thought I'd lie down. Nothing to worry about." He coughed and touched his chest.

Sammi Jo was not reassured. She placed her hand on his forehead. "You feel hot to me. I'm going to take your temperature."

Knowing how useless it was to try to dissuade her, Nate said, "While I lie here with the thermometer under my tongue, why don't you tell me how your hunt for a studio went?"

Sammi Jo agreed to this. "The hunt was a disaster. The first place used to be one of those little country stores out in the boondocks. The owner claimed it's been empty for only a year, but it looks as if it's been abandoned a lot longer. That is, by humans. I saw a number of signs that spiders, mice, and heaven only knows what other animals have taken it over. It would take me at least three weeks to get it cleaned up and then it would still need major renovation." She sighed and glanced at her watch.

"The second place looked all right from the outside, but the moment I stepped inside I almost gagged. The smell of cigarettes and stale beer must have seeped deep into the walls. I'm afraid that no amount of cleaning and painting would get rid of it." When Nate mumbled something around the thermometer, she added, "The place was a roadhouse for years. The Carolina Moon. Ever heard of it?" she asked as she took the thermometer from his mouth.

"I've heard of it. A rough place. Lots of fights. Don't know how often the sheriff had to go out there on Saturday nights." Nate watched her study the thermometer. "Well?" he asked.

"You have a fever. Almost a hundred and one. I'm calling the doctor."

"You don't have to. I'm probably just coming down with a cold."

Sammi Jo ignored his entreaties and phoned the doctor. When she returned to her grandfather's room, she carried a pitcher of water and a glass of orange juice.

"He said for you to stay in bed and drink lots of liquids. I'm to take your temperature and watch you. That means I better cancel my aerobics session at the church."

"No. Sammi Jo, I don't need a baby-sitter."

"I wasn't thinking of hiring a baby-sitter, but I can't leave you here alone."

"And you can't cancel this session. I won't let you."

"I don't see how you can prevent it."

"What if I get someone to come in to keep me company for an hour or so? Then you won't have to cancel, right?"

"Well, I guess. But only if it's someone responsible. Not Mr. Griffin. Half the time he doesn't remember where he lives."

"Agreed. Do we have a deal?"

"Yes. I'll go and fix some chicken soup," Sammi Jo said. "You rest."

By the time the doorbell rang, the fragrance of chicken soup filled the kitchen. Sammi Jo walked to the door, curious to see whom her grandfather had asked to stay with him.

She opened the door. In that first heart-stopping second she swayed toward Andy Rafe until her brain kicked in and she remembered what he had done. She reached for the door frame instead.

"My grandfather isn't feeling well," she said.

"I know. He called me."

"I might have known. The conspirators flock together."

"It was mostly me, so don't be too hard on Nate," he said.

"It's sweet of you to take the blame, but he told me all about it."

"But I'm the one who actually made the call."

"Are you proud of being a control freak?" she asked.

"I'm not a control freak," Andrew said, his voice mild. "I did what we thought needed to be done to protect you. And don't tell me you don't need protection or help. Everybody does sometimes. Nobody is so tough and so self-sufficient that they can go through life alone. Not even you, Sammi Jo."

Stung, she said, "I never claimed I could."

"Good. Then there's hope for us." Andrew smiled and then moved past her toward Nate's room.

Sammi Jo returned to the kitchen slowly, wondering why she had been tempted in that split second to fling her arms around Andy Rafe. It had been almost like a reflex. When had it become a natural thing for her to want to do that? Bemused, she filled a mug with chicken broth, placed it on a tray beside a glass of orange juice, and carried it to her grandfather. She was careful not to look at Andy Rafe.

"I want you to drink the broth. Then if you feel like having some broth with chicken and vegetables, I'm sure your co-conspirator will fetch you some. You're welcome to have some soup too," she told Andy Rafe. Despite her best intentions, her gaze met his. His hazel eyes held an expression that was partly amused, which annoyed her, partly desirous, which made her catch her breath, and partly warm and tender, which made her throat constrict. Blast the man.

Quickly she said, "I'll be back in about ninety minutes."

Because she had been an aerobics instructor for almost three years, Sammi Jo could lead the class while her thoughts flitted back and forth between her assorted problems. Predictably, they lingered on Andy Rafe.

Her grandfather was right. If she didn't care for that aggravating man, his high-handed summoning of the fire marshal wouldn't rankle nearly as much. Care for him? Wasn't that another word for. . . . Heaven help her. During a series of grapevines to the left, she realized, amazed, that she was a little in love with Andy Rafe. Maybe even more than a little.

Sammi Jo was so stunned by this discovery that she finished the aerobic segment on autopilot and didn't become fully aware that they had started the floor exercises until she heard the grunts and groans that always accompanied the ab crunches.

Drat! What a mess. She, who had sworn never to fall in love again, was in the process of doing so. Worse, she thought gloomily, it might be too late to halt this careening descent into emotional madness. What now? She had no idea.

The music segued into the relaxation mode. Sammi Jo pulled herself together. The women had worked hard and had earned the reward of deep relaxation. As she led them through the breathing and stretching exercises, she found herself relaxing as well, the first time all day.

When she reached home, their neighbor was waiting for her in the hall. After exchanging greetings, Mrs. Lawrence explained why she was there.

"Nate said you and your young man had to go somewhere, but you didn't want to leave him alone, so I came right over." She moved toward the kitchen and motioned to Sammi Jo to follow her. She whispered, "Have you notice Nate's cough? It comes from deep inside his chest. My husband sounded like that when he had bronchitis."

"I told the doctor about the cough and he said to phone him in the morning. Do you think I ought to call him again tonight?"

"No, dear. Morning will be soon enough, but you ought to put some eucalyptus salve on Nate's chest. That helped my husband."

"I don't have any. Where—"

"I have some. I'll get it for you when you come back. Don't look so worried. Nate'll be fine."

Sammi Jo tried to fix a cheerful expression on her face for her grandfather's sake before she entered the bedroom. "And where am I and *my young man* going?" she asked her grandfather pointedly. She flashed a severe look in Andy Rafe's direction but he merely lifted an eyebrow and shrugged.

"You're going to look at a possible location for your studio," Nate said. "You remember Mrs. Porter? Lives in that big mansion on Park Street?"

"Is she the one who wears those big hats with a scarf wound around the crown and sits two rows in front of us at church?"

"That's the one. Andrew will take you—" A coughing fit seized Nate. When it stopped, Sammi Jo lifted the glass of juice to his lips.

"Rest now," she said after he took a sip. "Andy Rafe will tell me all about it." She kissed her grandfather's forehead before she left.

On the way to the car she asked, "How did you find out about Mrs. Porter's house?"

"Nate remembered that most of those old mansions have a ballroom on the top floor."

"What makes you think Mrs. Porter would even consider renting out her top floor?"

"Because she's lived on a fixed income for the last twenty years and any extra money is like manna from heaven. And because Nate called her and asked if she'd rent her third floor to his granddaughter. She said she would."

Sammi Jo's face lit up. Then new worries wiped the happy expression off her face. "What?" Andrew asked.

"The ballroom is probably not big enough, and even if it is, does she realize how much noise we'd make?"

"I looked at it earlier today and it seemed big enough to me. The ballroom itself isn't as big as the space you had at that dilapidated Manning building, but it has several adjoining rooms which you could use for office space and dressing rooms. No more curtained-off areas. There's even a nice bathroom with a shower."

"Really?" she asked, her voice animated. "But the noise—"

"Mrs. Porter is as deaf as a fence post." Andrew grinned at her. "She told me she'll just turn off her hearing aid and you all can stomp around and make all the noise you want. She won't hear a thing."

"Does she have any idea how many people would be tromping up and down her stairs?"

"Not a problem. You can use the servants' entrance and staircase at the back. It's a little steep and rather narrow, but for people who take dance lessons and aerobic classes that shouldn't be a problem."

"Seems like you have thought of everything."

"I try to please my lady," Andrew said and bowed from the waist.

"By the way, who told my neighbor that you were my young man?" Sammi Jo demanded.

"Don't look at me. She came to that conclusion all by herself. I wouldn't dare to presume."

"Ha! You dare to presume a lot."

"It seems to me that I've been a model of reticence."

Sammi Jo almost choked on that statement. "You, who sicced the fire department on me?"

"Yes, but I haven't pressured you into my arms. And that is being reticent where it really counts, where restraint is really hard."

She mimicked playing a violin. "Poor baby." She smiled. "I feel sorry for you."

"That's better than you being angry. At least you're not tempted to throw something at me anymore. Of course, I haven't returned your bag yet to you either, so my claim may be premature," Andrew said with a return smile.

"Don't tempt me," she warned, but there was no anger in her voice. Odd how her fury had cooled.

Andrew opened the car door for her. As she slid past him, she brushed against his arm. Instantly warmth sizzled up her arm. Drat. Why was she so responsive to this man's touch? Even to his accidental touch? This was not only unfair, it was downright disheartening. Hadn't his offense been grievous enough to warrant a cold shoulder for at least a couple of days? She'd have to work on that.

The trip to Park Street had taken less than ten

minutes. The house could do with a new coat of paint, but other than that, Sammi Jo saw no signs of neglect.

Andrew introduced her to Mrs. Porter. They chatted a few minutes in the parlor. Then Mrs. Porter showed them the back staircase but declined to go up with them.

"You weren't kidding about the stairs being steep and narrow. I'll count the climb as part of the warm-up," Sammi Jo said.

"You aren't even breathing hard," Andrew observed.

"Neither are you."

"Stairs don't make me breathless. Only you do."

"Don't start being sweet to me, you traitor." Her voice didn't sound stern, she observed, chagrined. Half an hour with Andy Rafe and she was reduced to the toughness of a marshmallow. Sammi Jo gritted her teeth.

She stopped in the doorway of the ballroom and surveyed it.

"What do you think?" Andrew asked, suddenly feeling apprehensive.

"You were right. It isn't as large as my old studio, but it certainly is elegant. Look at the chandelier and the marble fireplace." She walked into the room and trailed her fingers over the smooth marble surface of the mantel. Then she touched the gold and beige wallpaper. "This looks like damask," she murmured. "And everything is clean. I wouldn't have to do any scrubbing or painting."

"Then you like it?"

"Of course. What's not to like? You should have seen the two places I looked at earlier today." She shuddered.

Encouraged, Andrew showed her the rooms which flanked the ballroom. "I thought these two rooms you could use for your clients to change in since they're next to the bathroom. The one on the other side you could use as your office."

She nodded.

Andrew watched her walk through the rooms three times, her expression a mixture of wonder and excitement. She executed some dance steps and nodded, pleased.

"Great. The floor doesn't creak." Then she turned slowly, taking it all in. "I think I'll hang the mirrors on this wall and place the stereo in front of the fireplace with the speakers on either side."

The oil painting above the fireplace caught her eye again. The woman, probably in her late twenties, wore a white lace dress and carried a basket filled with purple and yellow irises. "Who do you suppose she is?" Sammi Jo asked.

"Mrs. Porter's grandmother." When Sammi Jo looked at him questioningly, he added, "Mrs. Porter told me that when she showed me the room."

"I wonder what it would have been like to have lived in this house during her time?" Sammi Jo mused out loud.

"You would have hated it."

"Why?"

"Women were expected to get married and husbands had rights over their wives and children. If men were so inclined, they could be autocrats and exercise complete control."

"You're right. I would have hated it. But you—"

"I would have hated it too, whether you believe that or not. Women couldn't own property. They didn't even have the right to their own children. As a matter of fact, they had few legal rights. I can't stand such inequality before the law. It goes against everything I value." Andrew shrugged. "I'm sorry. I didn't meant to subject you to a lecture on my beliefs."

"No need to apologize. It's interesting to know what you believe in. At least what you believe in theoretically," she added meaningfully.

Andrew grimaced. "In practice I fell a little short. At least with you. In court I do much better." Frustrated, he added, "It's just when you add feelings, theory and objectivity sort of go out the window for men, and age-old, primitive urges take over. I'm not proud of that, but it happens."

"What sort of primitive urges?"

"Urges like, 'I have to protect my woman.' We, men that is, don't stop to ask if the woman wants to be protected. We leap into an action mode and charge ahead with sabers drawn. At least figuratively speaking." He paused, studying her face. "I promise I'll do better in the future. Please keep that in mind."

She nodded. Then, quickly returning to the business at hand, she said, "I hope you note that the room has two exits and the wiring and outlets seem okay, so you won't have to charge ahead and summon your friends from the fire department to evict me." She flicked him a telling look but her lips were almost curved into a smile. "Now the question is: can I afford the rent?"

"You can. It's the same as you paid the Mannings," Andrew told her.

"Really? How's that possible? This is so much nicer."

"Mrs. Porter was very happy with the amount I suggested."

"Hmm. Then I either overpaid the Mannings or I'll be shortchanging Mrs. Porter."

"The Mannings charged too much for what they offered you."

"Probably, but I was desperate to find a place, so they had me over a barrel." Sammi Jo looked around once more, a pleased smile on her face. "I better tell Mrs. Porter that I want her ballroom and ask her how soon I can have it."

She preceded Andy Rafe down the stairs.

Her new landlady told Sammi Jo that she could start her lessons any time she wanted. Since she had asked Lucinda to cancel lessons for the rest of the week, they agreed on Monday as the first day. Sammi Jo wrote a check, making the rental agreement binding.

All the way home, Sammi Jo was silent. Though she wasn't normally a chatterbox, Andrew sensed that her stillness was due to tension. As he walked her to her front door, he asked, "How worried are you about your grandfather?"

"I'm really worried. He hasn't completely recovered from his stroke. He's eighty-two. All illnesses are more serious at his age. And his fever is too high for this to be just a cold."

"Are you going to phone the doctor again before morning?"

"He told me it wouldn't be necessary unless Granddad's fever shot way up or he developed additional symptoms." Sammi Jo sighed. "If the doctor wouldn't think me completely hysterical, I'd call an ambulance and take Granddad to the hospital. Even if they couldn't do much for him right now, he'd be with people who'd know what to do if he got worse. I feel so helpless. What if I wait too long to get help?"

"Sammi Jo, his doctor didn't think hospitalization was necessary at this time. I know it's useless for me to tell you to relax, but you have to. For Nate's sake."

"I know." She took a deep breath. "I'll try to think positive. He's tough, isn't he? He'll be just fine." Her voice broke.

"Nate *is* tough. He'll be all right." Andrew put his hand on her shoulder in a comforting gesture. When she didn't shrug it off, he kept it there for a few precious seconds. "Now you put a smile on your face and tell Nate all about your new dance studio. He'll like that."

"Yes. Thank you, Andy Rafe."

"I owed you a new place. Good night, Sammi Jo."

She walked up to the porch.

"Sammi Jo, wait. I'll fetch your bag."

"Thanks. I do need it." She waited on the porch until he returned with it. "I'm sorry I threw it at you. That wasn't a mature thing to do."

"I acted like a Neanderthal, and you were angry. I'd rather you express your anger than go into a silent sulk."

"You don't have to worry about me sulking. That's too passive. Not my style."

"Good. I'll take my chances with you throwing stuff at me. I'm good at catching. That includes people when they stumble and fall. Good night, Sammi Jo. I'll call in the morning to see how Nate is."

"Good night." She opened the front door. Then she turned, wanting to call him back, but he had already walked away. A sense of longing swept through her that was almost unbearable.

Chapter Ten

Sammi Jo spent the night in the armchair next to her grandfather's bed. She put another pillow under his shoulders, which seemed to ease his breathing a little.

At seven the next morning she took his temperature and promptly called his doctor. Being the son of one of Nate's oldest friends, the doctor stopped at the house on his way to work.

Ten minutes later, she drove her grandfather to the hospital. That's where Andy Rafe found her later that morning, pacing back and forth outside her grandfather's room.

"How did you know we were here?" she asked.

"When I called and didn't get an answer, I looked up your neighbor's number. She told me you'd taken Nate to the hospital."

"The doctor says Granddad has pneumonia. They X-rayed his chest. Now they're running a test to see what kind of infection it is." She took a sip from a nearly empty paper cup.

Andrew took the cup from her shaky hand. "Let me get you some fresh coffee."

"No, no. I don't really need any more. I'm caffein-ated up to my scalp." She grimaced. "It also tastes awful."

"Have you eaten anything this morning?"

"No, I couldn't."

He believed her. She seemed ready to jump out of her skin.

"Did you know that pneumonia is the sixth most common cause of death in elderly males in the United States?" she asked, her voice as unsteady as her hands.

"Who told you that?"

"I looked it up in a medical encyclopedia during the night when I was trying to figure out what could be wrong with Granddad."

Andrew took both of her hands in his, forcing her to stop pacing. "Sammi Jo, since when is Nate just any elderly male living in the United States? This is a forceful man who's been active all his life. He is not about to give in to some measly case of pneumonia. Besides, did you look at the copyright date of the en-cyclopedia?"

When she shook her head, he said, "I bet those sta-tistics are out of date." Andrew had no idea if they were, but he knew he had to reassure her.

She pounced on his claim. "You think so?"

"Sure. Medical science is always making progress. Hard for encyclopedias to keep up. Some of their sta-tistics are bound to be out of date by the time they're printed."

"That makes sense," she said, her eyes pleading for this to be true.

"Of course it makes sense. Sammi Jo, take a couple of deep breaths," Andrew instructed, his voice gentle.

He kept holding her hands. He wasn't sure she even noticed, but she seemed to grow a little less anxious.

He kept one of her hands in his when the doctor came to speak to them. He could feel her tremble when they learned that Nate had bacterial pneumonia.

The doctor put Nate on massive antibiotics. When her grandfather didn't respond as quickly as they had hoped, they added oxygen therapy and artificial ventilation of his lungs. Though the doctor told Sammi Jo repeatedly to go home, she insisted on staying, going home only long enough to grab a few hours of fitful sleep, to shower, and to change her clothes.

Her parents came, carrying a big bouquet of artfully arranged yellow roses. Since her mother was acutely uncomfortable in the presence of illness, even her own father's, they didn't stay long, and Sammi Jo didn't mind their leaving.

Andy Rafe came twice a day. To tempt Nate into taking some nourishment, he brought low-fat milkshakes and tasty broths from the resort's kitchen. To help Sammi Jo get through the days at the hospital, he brought flowers, newspapers, and magazines.

Sammi Jo found herself looking forward to his arrival the way all of nature waits for the sunrise. One morning at seven-thirty she watched him approach, the morning paper under his arm, a bakery box in his hands. He wasn't wearing a suit as he had on previous visits, but jeans and a short-sleeved polo shirt.

"No court today?" she asked.

"It's Saturday."

"It is? I've lost all track of time."

Andrew studied her face. She looked utterly beautiful to him, though very pale. Her eyes had that feverish sheen to them that came from exhaustion and from running on nervous energy instead of food. The stress of Nate's illness was taking its toll. "Did you get any sleep last night?"

She shrugged. "Some. Off and on."

"Did you eat dinner?"

She furrowed her brow in thought. "I honestly can't remember. The days seem to run into one another."

Andrew set the box on the windowsill and laid his hands heavily on her shoulders. Squeezing them for emphasis, he said, "Sammi Jo, what am I going to do with you? You're going to collapse and end up being a patient yourself. Don't you know how that would worry Nate and slow his recovery?"

"You're right," she admitted, her expression contrite. "I'll try to do better about eating."

"Today you *will* eat. I'll make sure of that," Andrew told her. "How's Nate this morning?"

"I don't know. When I got here, the doctor was with him already. The nurse told me to wait out here. They've been in there for a small eternity. Do you think that means that my grandfather is worse?" Sammi Jo clutched his arm and looked at him, her face betraying the panic she was trying to hold at bay.

"No, I don't think it means that Nate is worse. Let's be optimistic." Andrew managed to smile at her. What he wouldn't give if he could ease her worries even a little bit. He felt powerless, a feeling he detested.

The doctor came out. When he saw them, he smiled. "Good morning. I have great news for you. Your grandfather is finally responding to the medication. His fever's gone."

"Thank heaven," Sammi Jo said, her face alight with joy.

"We'll keep him a few days longer to build up his strength, but then he can go home."

"Thank you, Doctor. Can I see him now?"

"Give the nurse a few minutes to finish what she's doing, and then you can go in. And get some rest," the doctor said in parting.

"I will," Sammi Jo promised. Then she turned to Andy Rafe. "Did you hear that? Granddad will be all right." She threw her arms around him, laughing and crying at the same time.

Andrew held her. He felt as if a great weight had been lifted. Nate would be fine and Sammi Jo was in his arms. Life couldn't get a whole lot better.

As soon as the nurse left, Sammi Jo rushed to her grandfather's side. He was sitting up in bed. She kissed his forehead which felt blissfully cool. She said a quick, silent prayer of thanks.

"I'm so glad to see you sitting up and looking better. You have no idea how worried we were. How are you feeling?"

"Like a truck ran over me a couple of times, but compared to how I felt yesterday, this is an improvement." Nate's gaze shifted from Sammi Jo to Andrew and back to her, but he made no comment. "I actually feel like eating something this morning."

"Say no more. I stopped at the bakery on my way over." Andrew opened the box and held it for Nate to see.

"I smell cinnamon. I've always liked everything that has cinnamon on it," Nate said.

"I can personally vouch for these cinnamon rolls." Andrew picked one up with a napkin and handed it to Nate. "Why don't I go and see if I can find us something to drink." Handing the box to Sammi Jo he said, "Help yourself. I'll be right back."

"Thanks." Sammi Jo chose a cinnamon roll too.

As soon as Andrew had left the room, Nate asked, "I'm glad to see that you and Andrew have patched things up." When she didn't say anything, he added, "You have, haven't you, Sammi Jo?"

"I'm not sure. We haven't talked about it, but Andy Rafe's been here at the hospital with me a lot. He's been supportive and helpful."

"You sound surprised by that."

"I am. I hadn't realized how much it meant to me to have him be here every day."

"Sammi Jo, it's all right to lean on someone every so often. It doesn't mean you're weak or dependent or anything else you modern women are so jittery about."

She shrugged, her expression a mixture of surprise and confusion. She had leaned on Andy Rafe, and it had felt good and right. Odd. She, who had resented all possessive, protective gestures by men, had liked them coming from him. What was happening to her?

"Give him a chance. Observing you two together, I think he's good for you."

Before she could reply, Andy Rafe returned, carrying three paper cups filled with orange juice.

"The hospital coffee looked like colored water and had absolutely no aroma, so I chose juice. I hope that's okay."

"Juice is actually better. All that lovely vitamin C will do us a lot of good," Sammi Jo said.

"Is that today's paper?" Nate asked. "What's been happening?"

Andrew handed the newspaper to Nate.

"Jumping juniper! The feud's started between the Mannings and the Whittakers?"

"Actually, it's ended already. They were arrested early this morning."

"Both groups?" Sammi Jo asked.

"We had them under surveillance and when they made their moves, we arrested them. However, not before the Whittakers engaged two black-and-white units in a high-speed pursuit."

"Is there enough evidence to put them away for a long time?" Sammi Jo asked.

"Thanks to your keen eyes, we got Junior and his cousin for auto theft and a bunch of related charges as well."

"Good riddance," Nate said and lowered the paper.

While he sipped his juice, Nate studied his granddaughter. "Sammi Jo, I don't want you to stay at the hospital today. You need to get some sleep. And eat a decent meal. You look like you've lost some weight, and you weren't carrying any extra pounds to begin with." Nate raised his hand when she started to object.

"Sugar, I'm feeling much better, but I suspect I'll do a lot of napping. There's no reason for you to watch me sleep. Go home. Rest and eat."

"Okay, but I'll be back this afternoon."

"No. This evening will be soon enough. I don't want to see you until you no longer look like you're going to keel over. Now go and let a sick, old man get some rest."

"For a sick, old man you're remarkably bossy."

Andrew reached for her hand and pulled her to her feet. "I'll see to it that she gets a decent meal and some sleep."

"You two are ganging up on me again. Aren't you ashamed, two men against one woman?"

"Not in the least. Not when the woman is you," Andrew said. "Even two against one, I suspect we're barely a match for you."

"Yeah, right." Sammi Jo kissed her grandfather and walked out with Andy Rafe.

As they passed the hospital cafeteria, Andrew said, "How about that meal I promised you?"

"Didn't you say a *decent* meal?"

"Right. How about lunch at the resort?"

"That's better."

"Since we have some time, how about getting some fresh air?" Andrew asked. "You've been cooped up inside for days."

"You're on."

In his car, Sammi Jo leaned back. All of a sudden she felt the tension drain from her. She sighed and closed her eyes.

"I'll stop to make lunch reservations. Does one o'clock suit you?" When she didn't respond, he looked at her more closely. Sammi Jo was fast asleep. For a moment he debated waking her to get the key to her house. Then he decided against it. She needed the rest. Andrew turned his car toward his house. She could sleep in his guest room until noon.

When Sammi Jo woke up suddenly from a deep sleep, her first thought was that her grandfather would be all right. She smiled and stretched. Her smile froze when she looked around and didn't recognize the room in which she found herself lying fully clothed on a bed.

The last thing she remembered was sitting in Andy

Rafe's car. Logically then, she had to be in his house. Her panic subsided. Walking down the hall, she passed the bathroom in which she'd spent that glorious half hour soaking in the hot tub.

She found Andy Rafe in the kitchen, putting something into the oven.

"I was about to wake you," he said. "How do you feel?"

"Groggy."

"I can fix that. The coffee should be about done." Andrew poured her a cup and waited for her to taste it. "How is it?"

"Delicious."

"It should be. You taught me how to make it."

"I don't remember how I got from your car into your house."

"I carried you."

"Why didn't you wake me? I could have walked."

"You looked like you needed the rest." Not to mention that he enjoyed carrying her in his arms. Instinctively, perhaps seeking warmth, she had curled against his chest. She had fit so naturally there.

Sammi Jo saw the clock on the wall and almost choked on her coffee. "Is that the right time? I had no idea it was this late. I need to get to the hospital."

"After we eat. I promised Nate that I'd feed you."

Sammi Jo sniffed the air. "Something Italian? It smells good."

"I ordered a pizza."

"That's nourishing, not to mention caloric."

"You don't have to worry about calories," Andrew assured her.

"Do you think my grandfather was right? Have I gotten thinner?"

"I can't tell from here. Come closer," Andrew said.

"How will being closer help you decide?" she asked but moved toward him.

He reached for her. "I can tell by touch when I put my arms around you." Andrew pulled her firmly against him. His hands caressed her back. "Hmm," he murmured.

"What does 'hmm' mean?"

"You definitely feel bonier."

"Bonier? That does it. Bring on the pizza," she said and gently pushed her hands against his chest.

Reluctantly he released her.

"What kind of pizza is it?"

"If I'd ordered just for me, I'd have asked for pepperoni, but since you're nutrition conscious, I asked for green peppers and mushrooms. We need our veggies," he said, his voice virtuous.

"I appreciate that," she said gravely, but when she saw the small chunks of green buried in the cheese, she chuckled. "I admire your notion of what constitutes a serving of vegetables."

"Hey, I tried." Andrew carried the pizza to the table where he'd set two places.

"Anything I can do?"

"Yeah. The salad's in the fridge. Bring it, please, and let's eat before the pizza gets cold."

Sammi Jo carried the salad bowl to the table. When she served it, she said, "I'm impressed. Three different kinds of lettuce, as well as radicchio."

"You suggested that I get different kinds. I listen when you talk to me, Sammi Jo."

Something in Andy Rafe's voice made her look at him. Something in his eyes made her heart skip a beat. She suddenly knew that something momentous would happen before the night was over. She had trouble swallowing, but knowing that he expected her to eat heartily, she forced herself to concentrate on the pizza. The only sound in the beautiful kitchen came from the radio, which Andy Rafe had tuned to an easy listening station.

"This is good pizza, but I can't possibly eat four slices." She slid the last piece onto his plate.

"Are you sure?"

She nodded and sipped her milk.

"Would you like a glass of wine? I served milk because I remember you saying that it was good for a dancer's bones."

"It's good for everyone's bones. This salad dressing is delicious. Did you make it?"

"The chef at the resort did."

"I'll have to teach you how to make dressing. It's simple and it's a shame this kitchen isn't used more."

"You can use it. I'd love for you to make it yours."

Sammi Jo put her fork down. "Exactly what does that mean?"

"Whatever you want it to mean," Andrew said.

"You want me to come over here to use your kitchen between dance lessons?"

"That would take too much of your time."

Sammi Jo got up to refill her glass. She didn't need the milk as much as she needed the time to think. "You want me to move in with you?" she asked.

"Yes. No. Both."

"Andy Rafe, that makes no sense, and you're usually a very analytical, logical man."

"True, except where you're concerned." He got up and came to stand before her. "How do you now feel about what I did? I know you were furious with me at first. Are you still?"

"No."

"Good. How do you feel about me? Do you trust me?"

Sammi Jo thought about that for a few seconds. "Mostly I trust you." When she saw his expression, she added, "I trust you except in circumstances where you think that I might be in danger. There I don't trust you not to interfere."

"You were worried to death about Nate. It's only natural to worry about people we care about."

"Worry, yes, but interfere?"

"Intervene, Sammi Jo, not interfere. There's a slight but important difference," he told her.

"And what you and Granddad did was intervene?"

"Yes. I know you hate being controlled and manipulated, but do you really believe you'd let me treat you like that? You're too strong a woman to stand for that." Andrew saw astonishment and the wonder of discovery in her expression. "You've grown up. No one is ever going to dominate you again."

"You're right," she said, pleased. "I am a strong woman. I wasn't when I got married, but I am now, so don't even try to control me. Not unless you're aching for a heck of a fight."

Andrew chuckled. "We'll probably have a few of those anyway, given our temperaments. But if we remember the bottom line, we'll come to a compromise and get a lot of enjoyment out of our reconciliations."

Sammi Jo's heart skipped a beat as she pictured those reconciliation scenes. Forcing herself to stay calm, she asked, "What's the bottom line?"

"That we can't help but be together. That when all's

said and done, we'd rather spend our lives together than apart. At least that's how I feel."

This time Sammi Jo's heart seemed to jump all the way into her throat. She felt a little light-headed. To steady herself, she laid her hands on his chest. Immediately he drew her closer.

"I told you once that most people call that feeling by another name," she murmured.

"Love?" He let the word hang tantalizingly between them.

"That's the word."

"I'll be brave and say it first. I love you, Sammi Jo. I probably have for a long time, and I probably always will love you." The light in her beautiful eyes told him how she felt, but Andrew forced himself to wait for her words. That is, if he could hear them over the tumultuous pounding of his blood.

"When I realized I was falling in love with you a few days ago, I was dismayed. Mostly because my one experience with that emotion was so painful. Now I realize that what I feel for you is different, stronger, undeniable, because you're a different kind of man, and I'm a different woman now too." She smiled at him, her love for him flowing over him like a lovely dance melody. "You know what, I'm so glad, so utterly grateful that this has happened. I love you, Andy Rafe."

Her words fell on him like a benediction. He buried his face in her hair until he could trust himself to speak. "Let me explain what I meant with that yes-and-no answer about living together. Of course I want you to come and live in my house. Nothing could make me happier."

"But?"

"But I don't want us to just cohabitate. I want this all legal and proper."

"You want a prenuptial agreement?"

"No!" Andrew said, shocked. "I find that much too cold-hearted and legalistic. What's mine is yours. I don't need a contract for that." He took a breath before he spoke again. "I need you to promise before God and the world that you'll be my wife for as long as we both shall live. Nothing less will do."

"You want us to get married. Why didn't you just say that?"

"Maybe I was afraid you'd say no."

"No chance. I shall be honored to make those promises before God and the world."

"Really?"

"Really. Speaking of promises, didn't I promise you nine kisses in a row? How many do I still owe you?"

"Five," he murmured.

"Ready to collect?" she whispered against his mouth.

"Am I ever."